HARRY MOON

First Light

by
Mark Andrew Poe

With Barry Napier

Illustrations by Christina Weidman

rabbit publishers

First Light (Harry Moon)
by Mark Andrew Poe
with Barry Napier
© Copyright 2018 by Mark Andrew Poe. All rights reserved.

Rabbit Publishers
1624 W. Northwest Highway
Arlington Heights, IL 60004

Illustrations by Christina Weidman
Cover design by Megan Black
Interior design by Lewis Design & Marketing
Creative Consultants: David Kirkpatrick, Thom Black, and Paul Lewis

ISBN: 978-1-943785-27-8

10 9 8 7 6 5 4 3 2 1

1. Fiction - Action and Adventure 2. Children's Fiction
Printed in U.S.A.

Welcome to the Place of Beginnings.

~ Rabbit

TABLE OF CONTENTS

PROLOGUE

Halloween visited the little town of Sleepy Hollow and never left.

Many moons ago, a sly and evil mayor found the powers of darkness helpful in building Sleepy Hollow into "Spooky Town," one of the country's most celebrated attractions. Now, years later, a young eighth-grade magician, Harry Moon, is chosen by the powers of light to do battle against the mayor and his evil consorts.

Welcome to the world of of Harry Moon. Darkness may have found a home in Sleepy Hollow, but if young Harry has anything to say about it, darkness will not be staying.

Family, Friends & Foes

Harry Moon

Harry is the thirteen-year-old hero of Sleepy Hollow. He is a gifted magician who is learning to use his abilities and understand what it means to possess the real magic.

An unlikely hero, Harry is shorter than his classmates and has a shock of inky, black hair. He loves his family and his town. Along with his friend Rabbit, Harry is determined to bring Sleepy Hollow back to its true and wholesome glory.

Rabbit

Now you see him. Now you don't. Rabbit is Harry Moon's friend. Some see him. Most can't.

Rabbit is a large, black-and-white, lop-eared Harlequin rabbit. As Harry has discovered, having a friend like Rabbit has its consequences. Never stingy with advice and counsel, Rabbit always has Harry's back as Harry battles the evil that has overtaken Sleepy Hollow.

Honey Moon

She's a ten-year-old, sassy spitfire. And she's Harry's little sister. Honey likes to say she goes where she is needed, and sometimes this takes her into the path of danger.

Honey never gives in and never gives up when it comes to righting a wrong. Honey always looks out for her friends. Honey does not like that her town has been plunged into a state of eternal Halloween and is even afraid of the evil she feels lurking all around. But if Honey has anything to say about it, evil will not be sticking around.

Samson Dupree

Samson is the enigmatic owner of the Sleepy Hollow Magic Shoppe. He is Harry's mentor and friend. When needed, Samson teaches Harry new tricks and helps him understand his gift of magic.

Samson arranged for Rabbit to become Harry's sidekick and friend. Samson is a timeless, eccentric man who wears purple robes, red slippers, and a gold crown. Sometimes, Samson shows up in mysterious ways. He even appeared to Harry's mother shortly after Harry's birth.

III

Mary Moon

Strong, fair, and spiritual, Mary Moon is Harry and Honey's mother. She is also mother to two-year-old Harvest. Mary is married to John Moon.

Mary is learning to understand Harry and his destiny. So far, she is doing a good job letting Harry and Honey fight life's battles. She's grateful that Rabbit has come alongside to support and counsel her. But like all moms, Mary often finds it difficult to let her children walk their own paths. Mary is a nurse at Sleepy Hollow Hospital.

John Moon

John is the dad. He's a bit of a nerd. He works as an IT professional, and sometimes, he thinks he would love it if his children followed in his footsteps. But he respects that Harry, Honey, and possibly Harvest will need to go their own way. John owns a classic sports car he calls Emma.

Titus Kligore

Titus is the mayor's son. He is a bully of the first degree but also quite conflicted when it comes to Harry. The two have managed to forge a tentative friendship, although Titus will assert his bully strength on Harry from time to time.

Titus is big. He towers over Harry. But in a kind of David vs. Goliath way, Harry has learned which tools are best to counteract Titus's assaults while most of the Sleepy Hollow kids fear him. Titus would probably rather not be a bully, but with a dad like Maximus Kligore, he feels trapped in the role.

Maximus Kligore

The epitome of evil, nastiness, and greed, Maximus Kligore is the mayor of Sleepy Hollow. To bring in the cash, Maximus turned the town into the nightmarish Halloween attraction it is today.

He commissions the evil-tinged celebrations in town. Maximus is planning to take Sleepy Hollow with him to Hell. But will he? He knows Harry Moon is a threat to his dastardly ways, and try as he might, he has yet to rid Harry from his evil plans.

Kligore lives on Folly Farm and owns most of the town, including the town newspaper.

GAINFUL EMPLOYMENT

E ven in a town where things are forever frozen in a state of near-Halloween, there's a certain magic that exists between young boys and lazy summer days. This magic is always a little more present in the afternoons. Especially when the sun starts to set and turns everything a shade of warm gold for about a minute or so.

Harry Moon was sitting on a park bench at the edge of the town square watching this very event on a Saturday afternoon. The setting sun traced a line across the tree tops of Wannapakee Canoe Camp and sent soft flares of light skipping along the tops of the buildings on Conical Hat Avenue. The fact that he was also munching on a grape PrestoPop Popsicle made the moment even more special.

His friends had scattered away an hour or so ago for dinner. Harry had, too, but had come back out to enjoy his delicious dessert and the beautiful summer evening scenery. The town was quiet at this hour. Most of the afternoon traffic had made it home to enjoy dinner, and the younger kids had been called inside by their parents. It was peaceful. It was beautiful. And it was one of Harry's favorite things about summer.

It was too bad school would start back in a few weeks and put an end to it all.

Just as Harry started to think about the first days of school and how he might finish out his summer vacation, a familiar bike came pedaling down Main Street. It pulled up alongside Harry's bench with a screeching of brakes and shuddering of tires. Declan Dickinson, one of Harry's best friends and a member of the Good Mischief Team, gave him a smile and a wave. He gracefully dismounted his bike and plopped down on the bench.

"What'cha doing?" Declan asked.

"Enjoying dessert and watching the sunset," Harry said.

"Yeah, I was thinking about grabbing some ice cream from the Screaming Jelly Bean," Declan said. "But look . . . Harry, I have a favor to ask."

"Sure. What do you need?"

It took Declan a while to respond, and Harry could tell that his friend was deeply troubled about something. Rather than pry, though, Harry let Declan work his way up to it.

"Well," Declan finally said, "I'm going to be gone for a week. Next week, in fact."

"That's a bummer," Harry said. "Why? What's up? Are you guys going on vacation or something?"

"Just Dad and I," Declan said. "I'm excited but . . . well, it's one of Dad's business trips, you know? So, I'll be hanging out in a hotel or the back corner of some dumb old conference center. That's the bad news. But the good news is that this trip is to Florida. Orlando, to be exact. And when Dad's business part of things is over, we're going to Disney World."

"That sounds awesome to me," Harry said. "Be sure to bring me back a *Star Wars* T-shirt."

"Dude, those shirts are like twenty-five bucks. It might be the most magical place on earth, but it's also the most expensive place on earth."

"I'll give you the cash," Harry said.

"No, it's no big deal. I'll get you one. I've got plenty of extra cash from my paper route."

"Thanks," Harry said.

"And speaking of my paper route, that's the favor I need to ask you. I need you to run my paper route for me while I'm gone. Mom said I can't go on this trip unless I find someone to fill in. She said she's certainly not getting up at four in the morning to drive around town just to deliver copies of *Awake in Sleepy Hollow*."

"Four o'clock?" Harry asked. Waking up so early sounded like cruel and unusual punishment as far as he was concerned.

"Yeah, it's really early. But Mom also said that I should probably ask you to do it. I really don't think she trusts any of my other friends."

It made Harry happy to hear that Mrs. Dickinson thought so highly of him, but he was still hung up on the whole waking-up-at-four thing. "Maybe being a good guy isn't such a good thing," Harry joked. "How many days?"

"Six mornings. I pick up the papers at four o'clock, and I'm usually done by six. You have to get the papers on people's driveways and porches before they open their door in the morning. I know it's crazy early, but honestly, it's sort of cool once you get the hang of it. You get to see first light."

"What's first light?" Harry asked.

"It's the time just before the sun comes up. You can't see the sun yet, only the light. It makes these crazy, creepy shadows. Your being a magic man, I think you'd love it."

"Really?"

"Really." Declan then leaned toward Harry and lowered his voice like he was sharing a very important secret. "I'm telling you, Harry. You will see things that will make the hair on your neck stand straight up. Some strange things go on in this town at first light. You have no idea!"

Harry munched thoughtfully on his Presto-Pop. He figured waking up early would be a nice way to learn responsibility. And this whole idea of first light sounded sort of cool. "Okay," he said, slurping the last of the popsicle from the stick. "I'll do it. Let's see what Sleepy Hollow looks like at first light."

"Awesome, Harry. Thanks so much!"

"Sure, no problem," Harry said. "But this is now going to cost you two shirts."

8

FIRST DAY ON THE JOB

By the time Sunday afternoon arrived, Harry found that he was no longer bothered by the idea of waking up at four o'clock in the morning. He figured if it wore him out, he'd just make up all of that missed sleep over the weekend. He'd been in the living room reading a book when he'd overheard his mother trying to secretly call Declan's mom. She'd asked about the route, whether it was safe or not, and for any pointers. By the end of the call, Mary Moon seemed just as excited to have gotten the job as Harry.

The Moon family had just finished washing the dishes from dinner when the phone rang in the kitchen. Harry's younger sister, Honey, answered it. She dashed to it in a way that had become normal for her lately. She was always complaining about how all of her friends had cell phones, but she didn't. She claimed it was unfair and embarrassing. Harry supposed that was why she was always so fast to dash to the phone when it rang. She was all about speaking on the phone now. It was something Mary Moon called a "rite of passage" for girls Honey's age.

When she called into the room for Harry moments later, she was clearly disappointed that the call was not for her. "Harry, it's for you!"

Harry took the phone and stepped into the

kitchen for some privacy. "Hello?"

"Hey, Harry," Declan said on the other end. "You ready for tomorrow?"

"I think so," Harry said. "I'm even going to bed early tonight to make sure I'm not too tired. Mom said I should try drinking some warm milk—that it might help me go to sleep easier. But I'm not too sure about that."

"Yeah, that sounds gross," Declan agreed. "Anyway, I wanted to go over the instructions with you. You know where the newspaper office is, right?"

11

"Yeah. It's on Main Street, right before you get to the cemetery."

"That's right. Now, you have to be there in the back parking lot right at four o'clock. Not a minute earlier and not a minute later. They are really strict about that. There will be three bundles of papers waiting for you by the back door. They should already be in a basket. What I do is just hang the basket from my

handlebars. It might make you sway a little at first, but it's easy to get used to."

"Okay. And how will I know who gets the paper and who doesn't?"

"Well, just about everyone gets the paper. There's a short list of people who I don't deliver to. They don't have a subscription. It's only like a dozen houses or so. I'll text you the names."

"Sounds good," Harry said. "Anything else?"

"Nope. I don't think so. But, like I said, keep your eyes and ears open. There are some weird things that take place in Sleepy Hollow before first light. You should get a real kick out of it."

"Thanks. Hey, have fun at Disney World."

"Oh, I will. Thanks again, Harry. You're a life saver."

The boys ended their call, and Harry marched upstairs, wondering how he was going to manage to fall asleep a whole hour and a half earlier than usual. Harry usually had no problems sleeping, but falling asleep so early was going to be hard. He was too excited, filled with questions and anticipation about taking over Declan's paper route for the week.

Maybe he'd have to try warm milk after all.

13

Fortunately, he was able to fall asleep without much of a problem. He drifted off a full hour before his usual bedtime with his trusty Elvis Gold alarm clock set to go off at 3:40.

∽

When the alarm clock went off, sounding out a few of Elvis Gold's catchphrases, Harry practically leaped out of bed. He had laid out his clothes last night. He slipped into them, too excited to realize that he was, in fact, still rather tired. He then dashed quietly to the upstairs bathroom where he brushed his teeth, applied deodorant, and ran a comb through his hair a few times.

He was downstairs at exactly 3:47. He slid two toaster pastries into the toaster and drank a glass of orange juice while he waited for them to pop up. The house was quiet all around him. It was so quiet that he could hear the fridge humming and the clock in the living room ticking. The pitch-black darkness of early morning pressed at the windows. Something about all of it *did* make him feel responsible. He was pretty sure he was getting to experience something that few others might never experience in their lives: the utter nothing that happens before 5:00 a.m.

His pastries popped up, and he wrapped them in a paper towel. With his juice finished, Harry headed out of the back door as quietly as he could. He hopped on his bike and pedaled out of the yard while munching on his breakfast. It was 3:54 when his bike tires touched the sidewalk. He knew he could make it from his house to the town square in about four minutes. And from the town square, the offices of *Awake in Sleepy Hollow* were surely no more than another minute or so. Knowing this, Harry didn't rush. He munched on his last toaster pastry, steering expertly with one hand. Besides, there was no big rush. Declan had told him to not arrive a single minute before four o'clock.

It took Harry very little time to discover that Declan hadn't been kidding. Sleepy Hollow seemed almost like a totally different town in the pre-dawn darkness. He felt like he was riding his bike across a very large stage where a play would soon be acted out. But for now, the set was not lit up, and the actors were not present. There was the flickering glow of the street lamps but even they did very little to drive away the darkness.

When he reached the town square, Harry looked up to the infamous Headless Horseman statue. He had to admit, it looked menacing in the darkness. Something about the shadows and the night surrounding it made the statue look like it might drop down onto the ground at any moment. Harry could easily imagine the large horse tearing through the streets while its decapitated rider howled with madness.

Suppressing a chill, Harry quickened his pace across the square, angling away from the statue. When he came out on the sidewalk on the other side, he could see the large glass window of the newspaper office. A small, decorative light on the inside of the window shone on the lettering on the glass: AWAKE IN SLEEPY HOLLOW.

Harry checked his watch. 3:59. He was going to be right on time. Not too bad for a kid that had never woken up so early in all his life.

He pedaled across the deserted street and felt like he was the only kid on the face of the planet. It was a lonely feeling but sort of cool too. He rode to the edge of the office and then turned down a small side road that led around to the back of the office. When he reached the open parking lot where cars would not be parked for another two or three hours, Harry checked his watch again and saw that it was exactly 4:00.

Feeling triumphant, Harry went to the back door and saw the basket of newspapers waiting for him. The papers were curled tightly and bound with rubber bands. There were three bundles, just like Declan had said. Harry estimated that there were somewhere around forty or so papers in each bundle.

He went to the wire basket the papers were in and picked it up. It wasn't quite as heavy as he had expected it to be so when he placed it over his handlebars, he felt rather strong. It did take some practice to drive in a straight line with the basket hanging from the front of the bike, but within a few minutes, Harry had the hang of it.

He sped out of the parking lot and headed down Main Street toward Mt. Sinai Road. His first house was down that way. Suddenly, Harry was a man on a mission. He had to deliver all of these papers all over town, and he had to have it done in a little less than two hours.

He gave the stacks of papers a knowing grin and put some more power into his legs as he pedaled farther into the darkness.

It wasn't until about 4:45 that Harry Moon saw the first traces of what Declan had referred to as *first light*. Really, it wasn't much like light at all. It was just a softer shade of darkness, almost like the night was starting to dissolve right along the horizon. Still, Harry noticed it right away as it started slightly behind him and to his right.

He had delivered exactly twenty-seven papers by then, mostly out on Mt. Sinai Road and a small section of Main Street before it intersected with Paul Revere Road. He was so focused on the lightening of the dark that he nearly missed his next delivery.

For most of the deliveries, he had simply tossed the papers onto the porches or directly at the front doors. But for this next stop, the porch was too far off the sidewalk. This was the Hanahan's house, which sat very far back off Paul Revere Road. He was going to have to get off his bike and walk up to the front door. He wasn't sure why, but this seemed almost wrong to him. As he crept down the sidewalk to their front door, Harry felt like he was trespassing.

He reached the porch and quietly climbed the stairs. He put the paper close enough to the door so the Hanahans could reach it without stepping out on the cold welcome mat. He knew he was being extra careful but didn't want to inconvenience anyone by accidentally

19

waking them up. Such consideration was just in his DNA; he simply couldn't help himself. Also, he did not want to wake their crazy dog—a mongrel named Snarl that had a bite and a bark that were both equally terrible and widely known throughout Sleepy Hollow.

With the Hanahan's paper delivered, Harry took a shortcut down Mayflower Road, which took him back around Main Street and directly toward Magic Row. Navigating the roads and streets in such a way made him feel like an explorer in some new, uncharted land.

On his way back toward Magic Row, he could better see the first light in the sky. The blackness that had sat on the horizon all night was now becoming a pretty shade of purple. There was also a muddy sort of gold color to it—two colors that didn't seem like they would go together but looked absolutely breathtaking in the morning sky.

The shadows of the trees and houses he passed seemed to stretch and almost breathe. As first light graced the town, Harry sensed a stirring of sorts—as if the town had been dead at night and was now coming alive.

With this feeling pushing him on to his next stop, he saw the first person on the streets that he had seen all morning. Harry squinted at the stores on Magic Row and let out a little gasp when he saw one of his good friends. It was Samson Dupree, fiddling with the door to the Sleepy Hollow Magic Shoppe. Before Harry could get close enough to call out to his friend, magic enthusiast, and mentor, Samson had unlocked the door and stepped inside.

As Harry neared his first stop on Magic Row, he checked his watch. It was 4:53.

"Four fifty-three?" Harry whispered to himself. "Where on earth would Samson be coming back from this late . . . or early?"

Maybe there's much more to Samson than I think I know, Harry thought. It was easy enough to believe. Samson was a great magician, and although Harry knew a great deal about him, he also felt that Samson was filled with secrets.

It was one of the reasons Harry always felt so drawn to the magic man.

He carried on with his morning, starting to worry that he might not have all the papers delivered in time. He worked a little faster, not allowing himself to be distracted by the beautiful sunrise that was overtaking Sleepy Hollow between five and six in the morning.

With dedication and some good old speed on the pedals, Harry finished Monday's paper route at 5:57. It was 6:00 on the dot when he guided his bike back into the rear parking lot of the newspaper office. There were still no cars there, and that part of town was still mostly quiet. A few cars made their way down the streets here and there, but there still wasn't much action.

Harry left the now-empty basket by the back door. He stared at the door for a moment, wondering what sort of work went into putting out a paper every single morning. He nearly reached out for the door to knock or maybe even try to open it, but he backed away.

Some instinct told him not to touch the door. And when it came to gut instincts, Harry Moon was usually pretty much on the money. He backed away, picked his bike back up, and started for home.

His first day of delivering papers to the people of Sleepy Hollow was all done. He had finished on time and without any hiccups. It had been one hundred percent successful.

As far as Harry Moon was concerned, that meant he deserved an early morning nap.

23

24

Second Breakfast

Although Harry had a nap in mind, his family had other plans when he arrived home. Mary Moon was cutting up strawberries for Harry's little brother, Harvest. His dad, John Moon, was pouring the first of his morning cups of coffee.

Wow, Harry thought. *Dad's first cup of coffee.*

And I've already been up for two hours. It was a thought that made him feel very grown-up—almost grown-up enough to try a cup of coffee. But not quite.

Amidst all of that, his folks wanted to know all about the morning's deliveries. How did it go? Were you tired? How many papers did you deliver? Did you see anyone?

So many questions, and all Harry wanted to do was return to bed and sleep for a few hours. But he did his best to answer their questions. He didn't want to seem too tired in front of them. He wanted them to think he was fully capable of handling the job and that waking up so early didn't bother him. His mother in particular seemed incredibly proud of him, and he didn't want to seem rude.

Still, when he thought about Honey up in her bed, not likely to come downstairs for at least another two hours, he couldn't help but be a little jealous. But at the same time, he was glad that he had this new experience—this new cool thing that was almost like a secret. He'd seen a side of Sleepy Hollow that few people ever got to see.

Harry ate a small bowl of cereal and then headed up to his room. He looked at his bed and realized that he really didn't want a nap at all. He was wide awake and looking forward to the day ahead. After all, it *was* summer vacation. He'd be with the rest of the Good Mischief Team within a few hours, and they'd

27

have the whole day ahead of them. He might get a little tired earlier than usual, but that was okay.

He went to his desk and started to doodle on a piece of paper. He started to think about seeing Samson unlocking his shop. *Why so early?* Harry wondered.

More than that, Harry had a very strong feeling that Samson wasn't just opening up his shop. He had been coming from somewhere and almost seemed a little secretive about it.

A shuffling noise from beside him broke his concentration. He looked in that direction and saw Rabbit trying to hop up on the desk. As always, Rabbit seemed to come out of nowhere. It was like some amazing magic trick where one minute there was nothing there and the next, there was an extremely wise talking rabbit.

Rabbit made it to the desktop with a single mighty bounce. His large feet landed on the desk gracefully.

"You're certainly up and at 'em earlier than usual," Rabbit said.

"Yeah. I sort of got a job."

"Really?" Rabbit asked.

"Yeah," Harry replied. He went on to tell Rabbit all about Declan's paper route and how he was filling in for the week. As he told Rabbit all about it, he wondered if he was wasting his time. Sometimes when he spoke to Rabbit, Harry got the feeling that Rabbit already knew everything he was saying. While listening to Harry's story, Rabbit pulled a carrot seemingly out of nowhere. He had no pockets anywhere on him (mainly because he didn't wear clothes), and Harry hadn't seen it on his furry friend when he'd hopped up on the desk. He simply chalked it up to yet another miraculous ability Rabbit kept in his bag of tricks.

"Sounds like fun," Rabbit said when Harry was done.

"Yeah, it sort of was. Hey, you might be able

29

to answer something for me!"

"Perhaps."

"I saw Samson going into his shop this morning," Harry said. "It was really early—just before five o'clock. And I know it might be a stretch, but I think he might have been coming back from somewhere."

"Samson is a man of many mysteries," Rabbit said. "Why do you think I'd know anything about him?"

"Well, you came from him. I mean, I know you were a gift for me, but you came from Samson's shop, right?"

"That's right. But while I consider Samson a good friend, I don't know *everything* about the man."

Harry thought about this for a minute. In the same way he thought Rabbit knew things before Harry mentioned them, he also suspected Rabbit spoke to him in riddles sometimes.

Rabbit had never given him an easy answer; he always made Harry work for his information, to figure things out using his mind. Maybe this was one of those times.

But honestly, Harry was a little too frazzled to go much deeper. Maybe waking up so early had thrown him off a bit. He was too sluggish to figure out Rabbit's riddles. He continued to doodle at his desk while Rabbit chewed thoughtfully on his carrot.

31

"You know," Harry said. "It's almost like a totally different town that early in the morning."

"In a good way or a bad way?" Rabbit asked.

"Both, I guess. But mostly good. Declan was telling me about this amazing phenomenon called first light. It's when the sun hasn't reached the horizon, but the sky starts to lighten anyways. You can almost feel night being pushed away by the day. It's so cool."

Harry was too preoccupied with his doodles to notice the knowing smile that touched the corners of Rabbit's mouth.

"Oh, I bet it is," Rabbit said, hiding the smile with his carrot.

The Secret Life of Sleepy Hollow

Harry woke up on Tuesday morning feeling like a seasoned pro. Now that he had the first morning of paper deliveries under his belt, he felt he knew what to expect. He also knew that he had just enough time to make it from his house to the newspaper offices, so he didn't rush as quickly when he got dressed and threw together a quick breakfast. This morning, it was some of his mom's leftover smoothie from yesterday and a banana.

He rode a little slower this morning but checked the time every minute or so. Taking his time, Harry was able to appreciate the silence of the town a bit more. Nightingale Lane was covered in shadows and eerily calm. He could hear the treads of his tires on the sidewalk and even the whispering noise the wind made as it sliced by him. Harry coasted along and smiled, feeling almost like he was floating in all the quiet.

Once again, he arrived at the back door of the newspaper office at exactly 4:00. The basket of papers was waiting for him. This morning, he didn't need any time to get used to the extra weight on the front of his bike.

He took the same route as yesterday, surprised at how quickly he had been able to bike around the entire town without the obstacle of traffic. Right away, he started tossing papers at the houses, making something of a sport of trying to get them to land squarely on the welcome mats. He wasn't quite that good yet, but he figured he'd be a pro at it by the end of the week.

Now that he was able to deliver the papers with a bit more confidence, Harry took the time to really study the finer details about the town as it sat beneath the last few minutes of pre-dawn darkness.

35

When he drove along the edge of the road down Mayflower Road, he noticed how the trees on the leaves seemed the blend into the darkness. It was pitch black beyond the first few trees, and Harry felt like he was staring out into absolutely nothing. He thought something like this should be scary, but it wasn't. In fact, it was rather peaceful.

He also noticed the low-lying mist that seemed to blanket the Sleepy Hollow Cemetery. Again, this was the thing of bad dreams and horror novels, but it did not scare Harry at all. It was simply the way the town looked while everyone was asleep. It was almost like the town had a life of its own when the sun went down—the secret life of Sleepy Hollow.

He wound through the roads, tossing papers and enjoying the solitude. When he noticed that he was approaching Scarlet Letter Lake, he listened extra carefully. Rumor had it that there was a monster living in the lake, and you could sometimes hear it splashing around at night. As he passed by the small parking lot and the lake's banks, he didn't hear a monster, but he did see something he had not expected.

There was an older man slowly guiding a wooden rowboat into the lake. The sight was so unexpected that Harry nearly crashed his bike into the ditch. Instead, he righted his course at the last moment and, unable to resist his curiosity, turned his bike into the parking lot.

The old man saw him pulling his bike closer. He waved to Harry and motioned him over. Harry did as he was asked, quickly pedaling over to the man and his rowboat.

"Hey there," the old man said. "What happened to Declan?"

The thought that Declan had seen this man before was sort of cool. He'd almost forgotten that Declan had noticed all of these things about Sleepy Hollow in the dark before he had.

"He's on vacation," Harry said. "I'm taking over for the week."

37

"Oh, good for you. It's peaceful out here at night, isn't it?"

"Oh, it sure is. Is that why you're out here so early?"

"Partly," the old man said. "I row out there a bit three times a week. You think it's quiet on the streets at this time of the morning? You should see how absolutely quiet and still it is out there on the water. I go out there to just be alone with my thoughts. It's peaceful."

"That sounds awesome," Harry said. He peered out to the dark water and couldn't even start to imagine what it might be like out there. A slight fog, similar to the one over the cemetery, was curling around over the water. It looked both inviting and terrifying at the same time.

"It is awesome, mostly," the man said with a chuckle. "But every now and then I get spooked. I don't know why . . . it's almost like something doesn't want me out there."

"Is it Scarlet, the Lake Monster?" Harry asked, getting excited.

The old man cackled so hard that he slapped at his knee. "Don't be silly," he said. "There's no lake monster out in Scarlet Letter Lake. It's just a . . . a feeling. Like something is trying to push me away from the water. It usually comes at first light."

"You know about first light?" Harry asked.

"Of course, I do," the old man said. "Some

people call it dawn, I guess."

Harry's excitement dwindled. Dawn wasn't the *first light* Harry was thinking of. Still, it was pretty cool that this old man rowed out to the middle of the lake several mornings each week. *And* he knew Declan. Harry couldn't wait to ask Declan questions about this strange old man.

"Well, enjoy the lake," Harry said. "I have to get the rest of these papers delivered."

39

"Take care, now," the old man said as he gave his boat one final heave. It careened into the water, and the old man hopped into it with surprising skill.

Harry gave the man a wave, staying long enough to watch him place an oar in the water and start rowing away. He then turned back toward Mayflower Road where he saw the very first signs of *true* first light appearing.

Just like yesterday, it was pretty hard to see at first. If he hadn't been looking for it, Harry thought he might have missed it altogether.

When he viewed it this morning, he thought of it as a curtain. The night itself was a curtain that was slowly being pulled up to reveal a whole different set of colors. Those colors were not the bright colors of the sunrise just yet, but a variety of colors that existed somewhere between light and dark.

Seeing this, Harry felt a little confused about what the old man had said. He had told Harry that there was a feeling just before dawn where he felt like something was pushing him away from the lake. For Harry, though, this true first light seemed to be very welcoming. It felt like it was accompanying Harry as he delivered the papers, encouraging him to do a good job and to pump the pedals faster.

So that's what Harry did. He picked up speed and tossed paper after paper at still-sleeping houses. Alongside him, first light continued to reveal itself as the curtain of night was slowly raised.

41

✑

Speaking to the man with the boat had set Harry behind by five precious minutes. To make up for it, Harry pedaled hard for the next several deliveries. He rocketed the bike toward Folly Farm Road, tossing papers like a machine. Only two mornings in and he was getting very good with his aim. He made a game out of how many front doors he could hit.

His throwing arm was getting a little sore as he rounded the corner at the intersection of

Folly Farm Road and Magic Row. He glanced at his phone tucked along the side of the newspaper basket and saw that it was 5:02. He was still a little behind compared to yesterday's time, but he thought he'd still be finished up by 6:00 if he really hauled butt.

As he reached into his basket for another paper, he caught sight of a person on the sidewalk up ahead. With the exception of the man on the lake, it was the first person he had seen out and about this morning, and he was not at all surprised to see that it was Samson.

This time, Harry just barely caught him as he was making his way through the door of the magic shop. The purple coat Samson always wore fluttered out behind him as the door closed.

Two mornings in a row? Harry thought. *Where on earth is he coming from at this time of morning?*

Harry was suddenly very interested in Samson's morning activities. He was so curious that he nearly stopped his bike by the front of the Sleepy Hollow Magic Shoppe to pay his friend a visit. But he was on a tight schedule. He'd already put himself behind by stopping to talk to the old man at the lake.

So, Harry went on his way, delivering papers and pushing his bike to breakneck speeds. Like the morning before, he was able to see the sunrise as he tossed his last few papers. When he headed back to the parking lot behind the newspaper offices, morning traffic had started to appear on the streets.

When Harry arrived to return the basket, it was 6:00 on the dot. When he pulled his bike to the back door, he saw that a single car had just finished parking in the lot. A woman stepped out. She was stout with silver hair. She turned and gave Harry a smile. It was Mrs. Mildred Middlemarch, the editor of the paper. She was holding a laptop bag and a very large cup of coffee.

"Harry Moon," she said as she approached the back door. "Declan told me you'd be covering for him while he was away. I was very happy to hear that you'd be his replacement."

"I'm glad I'm his replacement too," Harry said. "It's been a lot of fun so far."

"That's good to know," she said. "There's a lot more that goes into creating and delivering *Awake in Sleepy Hollow* than most people realize. I'm glad you're getting to see that and that you're enjoying it. I *do* certainly appreciate you stepping in for Declan this week."

"No problem," Harry said. "It's been fun so far."

Mrs. Middlemarch looked around the parking lot and then at her watch. "Well, you'd best be getting on," she said. "Please believe me when I say I'm not complaining, but try not to cut it so close for the rest of the week, okay?"

Harry thought this was an odd thing for her to say because he had been right on time. But he also noticed the look of concern in her eyes as she glanced around the parking lot.

"Can I ask you something?" he asked.

"Quickly, yes." She looked busy, a little scared about something, and in no mood for small talk.

"Declan said I could not be here any earlier than four in the morning and that I needed to finish no later than six. Why is that?"

"Well," Mrs. Middlemarch said. "The paper isn't even done being printed until nearly 3:30. And it takes twenty minutes or so for the employees to bind them all up for you. So, if you got here any earlier than four o'clock, the papers simply wouldn't be ready."

Again, Harry was confused. He was fairly certain that she was lying. He could tell by the way she refused to look at him while she spoke. Also, she seemed to be in a huge hurry to get out of the parking lot and inside.

"Oh, okay," Harry said, deciding not to push things any further. "Thanks. Have a nice day, Mrs. Middlemarch."

45

"Likewise," she said.

She then opened the back door and entered as quickly as she could. She closed it just as fast, leaving Harry alone in the parking lot.

He took a quick look around to see what could have possibly upset her but saw nothing. With a shrug, Harry got back on his bike and headed home with the sun continuing to rise in front of him.

PAPER BOY ON THE RUN

That night, Harry set the alarm on his
Elvis Gold alarm clock for an earlier time.
He gave himself an extra ten minutes
for the next morning. He did this for two
reasons. One, he wanted to arrive at the
Awake in Sleepy Hollow offices a little early
to see if Mrs. Middlemarch had been telling

him the truth, and two, he wanted to allow himself a few extra minutes to stop by the magic shop and ask Samson where he went in the mornings.

He fell asleep easily that night, feeling a little strange to be going to bed before Honey had even cut off her bedroom light down the hall.

Apparently, he had slept very well because when the Elvis Gold alarm clock loudly shouted presto and abracadabra, he was jerked awake at 3:20. Right away, Harry shot out of bed. It felt strange to be so well-rested at such an early hour, but as he brushed his teeth, he could not wait to get his day started. He made his way down to the kitchen as quietly as he could and threw together a bowl of cereal, which he slurped down quickly. After grabbing a cup of juice and granola bar, Harry was out of the house by 3:32.

He was quite proud of himself. Getting ready for the day in a hurry was easy. He didn't understand why his mom and Honey took forever in the morning.

He knew that it was only fifteen minutes earlier than the other two mornings he'd had the paper route, but it felt *waaay* darker. The town was like another world—like the dark side of the moon, drowned in darkness where no one lived. It was a little spooky but undeniably cool.

When he reached Main Street, he darted under the glow of the streetlamps. Overhead, he could hear all manner of summertime insects fighting for position under the glow of the bulbs. The town was so quiet; Harry felt like the bugs were speaking to him. *Good morning, Harry. Have a nice day, Harry. Gee, you're the best paperboy to have ever mounted a bike!*

49

As the *Awake in Sleepy Hollow* offices came into view, the conversation of the insects was forgotten. Now, all Harry could think about was what really went on at the paper before four o'clock.

It was 3:55 when he turned his bike onto

the side street that would take him behind the building. He came to a stop and quietly put his feet on the ground, pushing his bike into the darkness behind the newspaper office.

He was a little disappointed when all he saw was an empty parking lot and his basket sitting to the side of the door, empty. He did notice that the door was open, though. It was pushed about halfway open, spilling a bit of murky light into the parking lot. He quietly set his bike down and crept to the open door. Before he even looked inside, he could hear something that sounded like a very low humming.

He looked inside and froze in place. He saw two long tables, all covered in newspapers. Some of them had already been printed but others were blank. Standing over the blank ones were tall, menacing figures. They were dressed in dark robes, reaching out their murky hands with long fingers over the blank pages.

As they did this, they let out that humming noise Harry had heard outside. When they touched the blank pages, ink appeared on them. The ink came out of nowhere, and seeing it reminded Harry of a rumor he had once heard about how the papers in Sleepy Hollow were supposedly written in invisible ink.

That rumor now seemed to be true. But not only was the ink invisible, it was the stuff of magic. And, if he had to guess, not good magic. It was the magic Mayor Kligore used. These quiet robed figures were probably in his employ.

And now he knew why he was not supposed to be here before four o'clock. Slowly, he backed away. Maybe he'd just retreat to the town square for the next few minutes and come back when he was supposed to. Maybe he could—

51

As he backed away, his eyes still fixed inside the door, he accidentally nudged his bike. The noise it made was very small, but in the silence of the night, it was easy to hear. Inside the back room of *Awake in Sleepy Hollow*, the robed figures turned in his direction. From what Harry could tell, they had no faces, but he caught the tiniest flare of red from within the

dark emptiness of the hoods of their cloaks. Harry felt those red eyes staring at him as the hooded creatures came rushing out of the room with the papers momentarily forgotten.

Harry picked up his bike and jumped on it in a flash. He pumped the pedals right away, the tires churning under him. He looked over his shoulder and nearly screamed at what he saw. One of those robed figures was directly behind him. He did not see the figure's glowing red eyes because it was blocked by the gloomy-looking hand that was grasping at Harry. Harry pumped his pedals harder, barely getting away from the hand as it tried to grab him. He could actually feel the wind the hand left behind as it grasped for him—*that's* how close it was.

Harry reached Main Street and took a right. With the open sidewalk in front of him, he was able to pick up tremendous speed. Within a few seconds, the weird robed figures were lost in the darkness and shadows.

Not sure of where to go or what to do, Harry did a quick lap around the town square. The eyes of the Headless Horseman seemed to follow him. As he rounded the square, he started to feel guilty. Now he was going to let Declan down. After what he had seen, there was no way he'd be able to finish out the week. Those robed creeps would be on the lookout for him for sure.

As Harry finished the lap around the square, he saw a person walking down Main Street toward him The person's shadow was long, cast at a weird angle from the streetlamps. But as they stepped into the light of the street lamp closest to Harry, he recognized the person.

It was Mildred Middlemarch. She was hurrying toward him in that same nervous pace Harry had seen yesterday morning. She ran across Main Street, standing in front of Harry so that he could not steer around her.

54

"What are you doing?" she asked.

"I got there early this morning," Harry admitted. "I'm sorry. I just wanted to see what went on. And . . . well, now I know."

"We gave Declan that rule for a reason. It's a rule of the town. No one but myself and Mayor Kligore are allowed to see the papers being printed."

"But they weren't being *printed*," Harry said. "They were being . . . I don't even *know* what they were being. What were those robed things, anyway?"

"They work for the mayor," Mrs. Middlemarch said. "They're called the Quiet Ones."

"And they write *Awake in Sleepy Hollow?*"

"Sometimes they add to what I write. They sort of watch things happen around town and report it."

"Well, why is the writing of the town paper kept such a secret anyway?" Harry asked.

"The owner likes to keep it that way," she said. "It's been that way since I took over as editor ten years ago. But look . . . I have calmed them down. They understand that the papers need to get delivered. So, give then a few more minutes, and they'll be done. I have instructed them to leave you alone, and they will listen to me. You can pick up the papers without worrying about them."

"You're sure?" Harry asked.

"Yes," Mrs. Middlemarch said, already starting back across Main Street.

Harry believed her but, at the same time, was instantly suspicious. He had known that Mayor Kligore had a hand in the making of the town paper. But these new weirdos—the Quiet Ones—seemed like something darker than even Mayor Kligore was capable of. It also made him wonder just what sort of lies or made up stories he was delivering to the residents of Sleepy Hollow.

He was only a thirteen-year-old kid. Maybe he wasn't supposed to worry about those sorts of things. After all, he had promised Declan that he would cover his paper route while he was gone, so that was what he would do.

Still a bit nervous, Harry took another lap around the square in the dark before returning to the parking lot behind the newspaper office. When he arrived, the back door was closed, and his basket of newspapers was waiting for him. Harry quickly attached the basket to his handlebars. He looked around the parking lot in the same way Mrs. Middlemarch had yesterday morning. He could almost feel the red eyes of the Quiet Ones staring at him from

unseen shadows.

Harry sped out of the parking lot. His heart was pumping with fear as he started delivering the first few papers. He was nervous and scared, and, for the first time in a very long time, he felt slightly afraid of the dark.

He kept his eyes open for first light around the edge of the horizon, but even that would not distract him from the memory of the Quiet One that had come rushing after him, its deadly hand closing in inches from his shoulder.

57

It was a feeling Harry was not able to shake all morning. He was so panicked and out of sorts that he even forgot to check for Samson sneaking into the magic shop at such an early time.

When Harry dropped the empty basket off at the back door at 5:57, he had never felt so relieved. In the clean light of dawn, the parking lot was much less sinister, but Harry could still see those glowing red eyes under the hoods of the Quiet Ones.

Harry Moon headed back home on that third morning of delivering papers. He checked over his shoulder every now and then, fearing that something dark and sinister might be after him. Of course, there was no one following him. But he could still fell the red stares of the Quiet Ones crawling over him like a spider.

WONDER WOOD ROAD

On Thursday morning, the only reason Harry felt safe riding to the newspaper office was because Mrs. Middlemarch had basically given Harry her word that the Quiet Ones would leave him alone. To Harry, Mrs. Middlemarch always seemed conflicted, but when she said something, she meant it. She was a woman of her word.

He pedaled slowly through town toward the office, making certain he arrived right on time, just as the clock on his phone turned to 4:00. When he found the newspaper basket waiting for him and the back door closed, he was flooded with relief.

Man, what a chicken, he thought. He hated to admit when he was scared, but yeah, he had been afraid of what he might find waiting for him when he picked the papers up that morning.

With the basket attached to his handlebars, Harry started the morning. It was hard to believe that he was more than halfway through with the week. It had gone by a lot faster than he had expected, and he was really going to miss the paper route. It was more than just the sense of responsibility. He was also going to miss the feeling that he had the entire town to himself for that little block of time.

It was Thursday morning. It was his fourth

morning delivering papers. He still found wonder and beauty in the quiet darkness of the town, but he was used to it now. His thoughts were more focused, and he was able to let his mind wander. He wondered how Declan's vacation was going. He wondered if there might be a job for him delivering papers later in the year. Maybe he and Declan could split the route up or something.

He also thought about the Quiet Ones and Mrs. Middlemarch. He wondered what the working relationship was like between her and Mayor Kligore. It made him feel a little sad for Mrs. Middlemarch. It must be terrible to work with Kligore. He knew that many rumors around town speculated that the paper was written with invisible ink. This was so the stories and articles would disappear within a day, making sure there was never any written record of their cursed little town.

Harry thought these things while tossing papers. He hit every door dead center. He was focused. He was a man on a mission—a boy on a bike and a magician with meaning.

61

He had a job to do. By goodness, he was going to do it well.

But, suddenly, his thoughts seemed to soften. It was weird, really. Sometimes his mom would catch him staring off into space, thinking about boy things. She'd ask him what he was thinking about and he'd say nothing, which was usually true. Mary Moon called it *zoning out*. And that's how Harry felt in that moment as the focused

concentration and thoughts seemed to slip out of his head. It was such a strong feeling that he wouldn't have been surprised if he looked down at the road and saw all of his thoughts lying there in a pool, having slipped from his ears.

Harry brought his bike to a stop. The feeling wasn't a bad one but was sort of cool and peaceful. His heart fluttered a bit, and for reasons he could not explain, he felt misty-eyed. He looked ahead and saw that he was approaching Wonder Wood Road. And in that direction, he could see what Declan had referred to as first light quite clearly—clearer than he had seen it all week.

63

Once, he'd attended an art show with Honey and watched a man paint a forest scene. The painter had explained that the first thing he did was paint the entire canvas a shade of very dark purple, so dark that it was almost black. He then started to create weird smudges with the edge of a sponge. Those smudges somehow became trees on the painting. Harry had been blown away by how simple yet pretty it had been.

That was sort of how he felt as he stood with his bike between his legs at the start of Wonder Wood Road. First light was creeping upward through the trees. It was almost as if the road itself was causing it, creating a whole new sky. The faded black of the pre-dawn darkness was no different than he'd seen it Monday through Wednesday. The colors were all the same. But he was seeing it more clearly than ever.

Watching it, Harry thought it looked like a living, breathing thing. He knew it was just the sky growing lighter because the sun would soon be rising, but he got the sense that it was somehow alive.

That was silly, though. Still, he could not deny how it made him feel: the indescribable flutter in his heart, as if it were trying to float out of his body; the weird tears brimming at the corners of his eyes.

And, as odd as it seemed, Harry thought he could also *hear* it. It sighed through the trees, and when it touched his ears, it was almost like hearing a beautiful angel singing, lost out in the forest somewhere.

Unable to resist the feeling that seemed to be glowing inside of him, Harry started forward down Wonder Wood Road. The paper route was forgotten for the morning. Besides, there were only two paper subscribers down Wonder Wood Road. In that moment, Harry was only focused on first light. He could sense it all around him as the sky continued to lighten even though it was still quite dark.

A smile covered his face, and he wasn't sure why. But he continued to pedal, sensing that there was something up ahead. *Maybe, he thought, there's some answer to what first light really is.*

That thought alone made him want to pedal harder. He nearly did, standing on the pedals and leaning forward to get the maximum amount of speed out of his trusty bike. But as soon as he gripped the handlebars, the feeling that had made him feel lighter than air was gone.

In its place was another feeling. This one was nearly the exact opposite of the one he'd just experienced. It came almost like a voice that filled his head, and it gave a very simple command.

Stop. Turn back.

The voice or thought or whatever it was struck him so suddenly that Harry again stopped his bike. He peered ahead farther down Wonder Wood Road, badly wanting to continue in that direction. But he felt something else coming from that direction, something that did not want him there. In turn, it made Harry not want to be there. It sent a bolt of fear through him that made him want to turn and run.

Slowly, Harry started to feel that fear fill him. It was almost like the feeling he'd had when he thought the Quiet Ones had been chasing after him for a second time yesterday morning.

Harry tried to find that overpowering feeling of joy again, but it wasn't anywhere to be found. The tears were no longer in his eyes, and his heart no longer seemed to be flying. Instead, it felt like it might actually be sinking.

Confused, Harry turned his bike around. First light was disappearing all around him as true dawn started to peek up over the horizon. He thought of the old man out at Scarlett Letter Lake yesterday. Hadn't he said something about feeling very happy out in the center of the lake but also getting the sense of something pushing him away?

67

That's exactly how Harry felt as he headed back to town to finish his route.

He looked back down Wonder Wood Road one more time and was sad when he realized that it was just a plain old road. Whatever sense of magic he'd felt from it moments ago was gone. Even the sense of fear was gone. So was the demanding thought that had not been his own that had instructed him to turn around.

Harry left it all behind, reaching into the basket for the next paper to be delivered. Behind him, the sun graced the day, and Harry

Moon slowly started to forget about the beautiful feeling that had enveloped him for a moment out on Wonder Wood Road.

∽

He'd only lost about three minutes, so he wasn't in much of a rush to catch up on his time. However, when he reached Magic Row, he remembered that he'd wanted to try to catch up with Samson before he snuck into his shop. But luck wasn't in Harry's favor. Once again, he was too far away from the magic shop when he saw Samson unlocking the door and walking inside.

Harry thought about yelling out for Samson but didn't think it would be a good idea. It was only 5:02 in the morning. Yelling out in the middle of the street might wake quite a few people up and cause tempers to flare.

I'll just swing by the shop some other time, Harry thought. Yet the mystery of where Samson went so early in the morning (or, rather, where he was coming back from so late) kept plucking at Harry's brain.

As Sleepy Hollow slowly became washed in morning sunlight, Harry finished up his route for Thursday morning. He managed to finish eight minutes early. He spent those eight minutes circling back around toward Wonder Wood Road. He wondered if he might get that feeling again—that feeling of peace and being bowled over by whatever magical power first light seemed to have.

69

As he suspected, though, he felt nothing when he came to Wonder Wood Road. The sun was now completely up, and the trees bordering the road looked plain and simple. If there had been anything magical out here during first light, it was gone now. Harry stood at the edge of the road with his bike between his legs, waiting—but there was nothing.

A little disappointed, Harry turned his bike around and headed back to the *Awake in Sleepy Hollow* offices. It was 6:01 when he dropped the empty basket off by the back door. When he turned to leave, he paused at the opening of the parking lot. He watched the back door and the basket, wondering why he had to have the basket delivered by a certain time.

It took no more than thirty seconds before the back door opened and an arm emerged. The arm was covered in a black robe. A gnarled pale hand with long thin fingers snatched the basket up.

A Quiet One, Harry thought with a shudder.

Just as soon as the robed arm appeared, it drew back into the building and closed the back door behind it.

An uneasy feeling churned in Harry's guts. Something about the mere idea of those Quiet Ones did not sit well with him. They felt dark and evil. And as a boy that practiced the Deep Magic, he had something of a radar for evil things.

Maybe Samson knows more about them, Harry thought. *That's yet another reason to pay him a visit.*

Harry steered his bike back toward the magic shop. He propped his bike against the side of the shop and tried opening the door. He wasn't too surprised to find it locked. After all, there was still another three hours before Samson usually opened up his shop for business.

Confused and a little scared, Harry got back on his bike and headed home. As he turned onto Nightingale Lane, he looked to his left. Wonder Wood Road was down that way, and even now, Harry thought he felt the place calling to him.

He wasn't quite sure if that was a good thing or not.

With more questions than ever about Sleepy Hollow, first light, and his good friend Samson Dupree, Harry pedaled home.

12

The Right (and Wrong) Questions

When Harry arrived home, his family was sitting around the breakfast table. And while the smell of pancakes and syrup was enticing, Harry realized that he was quite tired. More than that, he was confused. He needed some time alone to process everything he had seen and experienced over the course of the last four mornings.

"Are you sure you don't want at least one pancake?" Mary Moon asked him.

"No, thanks," he said. "I think I'm going to take a quick nap."

"Okay," she said. "Whatever we don't eat, I'll wrap up and leave in the fridge for later. But with the way Harvest is putting them down, I can't guarantee anything."

Harvest chuckled in response as he rolled a sticky pancake up like a burrito and gobbled half of it in one bite.

"Thanks, Mom," Harry said.

He went upstairs and wasted no time crashing in bed. He kicked his shoes off and stared up at the ceiling. He was confused about how he had felt such a peaceful and loving feeling an hour and a half ago on Wonder Wood Road and now felt sort of . . . sort of *blah*.

His mind was going in a bazillion directions at once. Was that *true* first light he had seen on Wonder Wood Road, and if so, what was that feeling it had sent rushing through him?

What were the Quiet Ones up to, and was Mrs. Middlemarch being held as the editor of *Awake in Sleepy Hollow* against her will? Harry doubted this because she seemed to be able to order the Quiet Ones around.

75

What secret was Samson holding about why he went into the magic shop so early in the morning? And if Samson *was* keeping a secret, would he maybe share it with him?

With so many questions in his head, Harry was unable to take the nap he wanted. After a while, he sat up in bed. *Might as well head down to get some of those leftover pancakes,* he thought.

As he was about to roll out of bed,

Rabbit hopped up onto the mattress. Harry wasn't quite sure where he had come from. It was one of the many things that made Harry's special friend so unique.

"How's the paper route going?" Rabbit asked.

"Delivering the papers is really fun," Harry said. "But . . . well, I don't know. At first being the only one to see the town at that time of day was cool. But now I'm noticing a lot of things that I don't understand."

"Like what?" Rabbit asked.

Harry told him about his encounter with the Quiet Ones yesterday, as well as the brief conversation he'd had with Mildred Middlemarch. He then tried his best to explain the conflicting feelings he'd had on Wonder Wood Road—from feeling so happy and peaceful that he had nearly cried to sensing a strong thought in his head telling him to stop and turn back.

"And then there's Samson," Harry said.

"What about him?"

"Well, I know it's none of my business, but I don't understand why he sneaks into the magic shop so early every morning."

"Maybe he just really likes this work?" Rabbit suggested. Sometime between leaping up on the bed and now, he had produced another carrot from somewhere. Seeing the mystery carrot made Harry smile.

"I'm sure he does," Harry said. "But I get the feeling that he's coming back from somewhere. Like he's been out doing something and doesn't want anyone to know about it."

Rabbit said nothing to this. He just looked at Harry, waiting to see if his human friend had any other thoughts on the matter.

"So where do you think he goes?" Harry asked Rabbit. "Do you have any idea?"

Rabbit licked some carrot flecks off his paw. He thought very carefully before giving his answer. "Maybe I do. Just maybe I do. Who wants to know?"

"I do."

"Why? Just curious? You know, you have to be careful when you ask questions, Harry Moon. Sometimes the answers take you places you don't intend to go."

Harry looked intently at Rabbit. "Oh no. Is Samson involved in something he shouldn't be?

Is that why he is out after dark? He can't be. He's Samson!"

"Oh, come on now," Rabbit said, shaking his head. "What do you think? That's not what I meant. This is Samson we're talking about here. What you need to understand is that when you ask a question, the answer sometimes will change you. You have to be ready for that if you are searching for the Deep Magic."

"I am always ready for the Deep Magic," Harry said, a little excited now.

19

Rabbit hopped off the bed and looked up at Harry. "Then ask him. And then let go. This is one reply that you might not be expecting."

"I don't know what you mean," Harry said.

"I know," Rabbit said. "But this is an answer I think you need to figure out on your own. Go talk to Samson. But not until you know you're ready for what he has to say."

On two different occasions later that day, Harry nearly went by the Sleepy Hollow Magic Shoppe to speak with Samson. He actually strolled by it once and reached out for the door handle. But something Rabbit had said spooked him. Harry had always known that Samson and Rabbit were linked somehow, so if Rabbit thought the answers might change him, Harry thought it might be best to wait.

Tomorrow. I'll visit him tomorrow right after he opens the shop.

He did his best to spend the rest of the day like any other thirteen-year-old boy during the end of summer vacation. He hung out with his friends, wandering here and there to do what boys typically did. He hooked up with Bailey and Hao, the other members of the Good Mischief Team, and walked around the woods behind Magic Row. They skipped rocks on the creek behind Wannapakee Canoe Camp. They had lunch under a gazebo in the town square, wolfing down hotdogs, fries, and milkshakes from Burger Heaven.

As dinnertime rolled around, the three boys were sitting idly on a small bench beside the town hall. They were chitchatting about what school would be like as freshmen in high school. It was almost here! Harry's phone rang. He checked the display and saw that it was Declan calling to FaceTime with him.

Harry accepted the FaceTime call as Bailey and Hao crowded in around him to see their friend. Declan appeared on the screen, sitting in front of a cool, majestic-looking castle. He was wearing a set of Mickey Mouse ears, and his lips were caked with some sort of ice cream. He looked positively happy but also a little tired.

81

"Declan!" the three boys shouted at once.

"What are you geeks doing?" Declan asked.

"Just sitting around doing nothing," Hao said. "What about you?"

"Having a blast! I rode Space Mountain like eight times. And I got my picture with Peter Pan and the Mad Hatter!"

"Sounds awesome," Bailey said.

"And Harry, I got those shirts for you," Declan said.

Harry had nearly forgotten about the shirt he'd requested from Declan when he had taken on the paper route job. "Thanks, man."

"How's the paper route going?"

Harry didn't mean to, but he hesitated before he answered. There was so much he wanted to say, so much he wanted to ask. But because Bailey and Hao were there with him, he kept it simple. "It's going great," he said. "I'm having a blast."

"That's great," Declan said. "I really wish you guys could be here. It's tons of fun. Dad is cool and all, but he just about hurled on the Tea Cups."

The boys had a laugh at this image, but Harry's thoughts had once again turned to the things he had encountered on his paper route.

He couldn't wait for Declan to get back home so they could compare stories.

"Well, I have to go, guys. I'm going to try to squeeze in one more ride on Space Mountain before we have to leave."

All three of the other boys gave loud shouts of goodbye. Harry then ended the call, and the Good Mischief Team was silent for a while. Harry was pretty sure Bailey and Hao were quiet because they were bummed, wishing they were at Disney with Declan. But Harry had fallen silent because he could not get his thoughts off the paper route and all the questions he had.

That's it, he thought. *I'm going to go talk to Samson tomorrow. I have two more days of the paper route, and if I don't get some answers pretty soon, I may go bonkers before Saturday's final delivery!*

"Guys, I'm going to head home," Harry said. "That paper route has me getting to bed early."

"But it's not even dinner time yet," Bailey quickly pointed out.

"I know. I'm just tired. I'll catch up with you guys tomorrow."

They waved Harry off as he started walking in the direction of Nightingale Lane. Harry took a final look back before he headed home, looking farther down Magic Row where Samson's shop sat like a lighthouse for him.

He could go there now, and he was sure Samson would be glad to see him. But the conversation he'd had with Rabbit made him want to wait.

"This is one answer that you might not be expecting." That's exactly what Rabbit had said, and something about that seemed odd to Harry.

Still, he had made the decision: he'd go see Samson tomorrow. And in making that prom-ise to himself, Harry found that he was very anxious for tomorrow to come.

SAMSON DUPREE, PAST AND PRESENT

Thursday afternoon became Thursday night, and sometime after all of the lights went out in the Moon household, Thursday night became the very early hours of Friday morning. Mary Moon had not slept well all night. She'd woken up from time to time and looked at the clock. She woke up once at 11:27, then again at 1:15, and then again at 3:07.

She was restless and had no real idea why. She looked up at the ceiling, waiting for Harry to start his early day. She could hear his Elvis Gold alarm clock go off. After that she lay still in her bed, listening to Harry working his way through the house in the still dark early hours of the morning. She pulled the covers up tight to her chin.

It was easy to tell where Harry was within the house. The refrigerator door with its tiny squeak and the wooden floor in the hallway told her exactly where Harry was as he clattered about getting ready for his paper route. Harry never ever turned a light on. He knew his way around in the dark like he had flashlights for eyes. It was just one of the very special things about her son.

A few minutes later, she heard the back door open. The screen door quietly clicked against the house. She smiled into her pillow because she knew Harry was being careful not to wake his family as his bike pinged over the pebbles and faded off into the night.

What Harry didn't know—what he would *never* know—was that his mother was always worried about him. The unusual bond Mary Moon had with Harry was different than anything she had ever experienced in her life. Of course, she loved the other children totally and completely. There was never any question about that. It was just that Harry was different. Mary had felt it from the very first moment Harry had been placed into her arms and she tightened his tiny blanket while snuggling Harry into a tiny package. She had known in that first moment that she was somehow a part of her little boy's very special and unique journey.

87

She turned over and tried to go back to sleep. It was hard to do. She didn't like Harry out by himself in the dark. The dark frightened her.

But it also stirred a memory out of her

sleepy brain. It came as a voice first, a series of words tugging the rest of the memory along with it.

"Don't see you much outside after dark."

Mary Moon remembered the exchange Samson had spoken to her when she first moved back to Sleepy Hollow. She and John Moon took over the home her great aunt had once owned. Mary was walking through the town square. It was twilight. It was then that she ran into Samson.

Samson's words about Harry that night had haunted her for several years.

"Your son will learn to find his way around the dark," Samson had told her. "He can use your help in the beginning. It will be part of what makes him special. It will be a valuable gift he will bring to others."

"What does that mean?" asked Mary. "I don't really feel comfortable in the dark."

She would always remember Samson's next words. Even as he spoke them to her on that night years ago, she'd felt like they had imprinted on her heart. "It's not about the dark, Mary Moon," he had said. "It's about the eyes. Harry has the eyes to see what is hidden by the dark. His town is waiting for him. They are weary of this crazy Halloween business the mayor has brought to its streets. Secretly, they do not like the shadow Kligore has cast across the Hollow. They are groaning for someone to release them from the shroud of darkness they awaken to every morning."

89

Samson looked at Mary Moon and smiled softly. "They are waiting for your son."

"But he's only a baby," she had protested. "He's only a little boy."

Samson nodded. "And he always will be. Harry will always have the heart of a child even as he grows into a strong young man. It is his forever child's eyes that give him sight in the night. And because of that, you should be relieved. Don't be afraid of the dark, Mary Moon."

It was amazing how that memory put her at peace. It allowed her to relax as she pulled the blankets even closer and tightened her eyes as she snuggled up against her husband.

Although she felt safer and more at ease now, Mary Moon was still not able to go back to sleep. She remained awake in the dark until the rest of her family started to stir, making morning noises to start the day.

∽

Harry hit every front door on Friday morning with the exception of the Hanahan residence. And that was only because their house was so stinking far off of Mayflower Road. During Friday's route, he sped by Scarlett Letter Lake, hoping to see the old man with the row boat. But he was nowhere to be found. The lake was still, quiet, and covered in a blanket of morning darkness. It was very pretty but didn't come close to what he had experienced out on Wonder Wood Road.

Harry thought about hanging out on Wonder

Wood Road, hoping to experience the sensation that first light had sent through him yesterday. He decided not to because he could clearly recall that demanding and almost booming voice that had swept through his head like a rough wind.

Stop. Turn back.

Just thinking about that thought or voice or whatever it had been gave Harry the creeps. So, he steered clear of Wonder Wood Road, only venturing down it to deliver the two papers for the subscribers that lived there.

When first light appeared, Harry was zipping down Folly Farm Road, back toward Magic Row and Main Street. As usual, first light was an awesome sight to behold, but it was nothing compared to yesterday's sighting. Harry wondered what it was about Wonder Wood Road that had made it so special. He was wondering this when he made his way onto Magic Row. He did not see Samson entering the magic shop this morning, but when he passed the shop, Harry did notice a light was on somewhere inside.

Soon. I just need to finish the route first.

Harry completed the morning route. He dropped the empty basket off at 6:00 on the dot. When he placed the basket by the back door, Mildred Middlemarch's car pulled into the parking lot. When she got out of the car, she looked in a better mood than the last time she had seen him.

"I have to tell you," she said. "You're doing a fantastic job, Harry Moon. It took Declan a few weeks to get the hang of the two-hour delivery time. But you're knocking it out of the park."

"Thanks," Harry said.

"And I hope there are no hard feelings about the other morning. The Quiet Ones . . . well they don't think before they act."

"Do they work for Mayor Kligore?" Harry asked. He hadn't *meant* to ask the question, but it popped out of his mouth before he could stop it.

Mrs. Middlemarch looked a little scared that he had even asked. She said nothing. She simply sighed. Harry understood her answer hidden in her silence.

"Do they scare you sometimes?" Harry asked. "Do they hurt you?"

"Well, they certainly aren't any fun to look at, now, are they? But no, they do not hurt me. They are just . . . you know, Harry, I really shouldn't be talking to you about this."

93

Harry nodded. He understood. He just wished she would have kept talking so he could have asked her if all the stuff he'd heard about the newspaper and the invisible ink was true. But she already looked freaked out, so he politely kept quiet.

"I understand," he said.

"So, tomorrow is your last day," she said, hurrying to the back door. "We'll mail your check to your home address. Is that okay?"

"Sure," Harry said, hopping back on his bike and heading back out to Main Street. He gave her a wave, but she did not return it. She was already heading inside the office with the door closing behind her.

Harry checked the clock on his phone: 6:08. He had originally planned to stop by the magic shop later in the day, during business hours. But he was just too anxious. He couldn't wait any longer. Rabbit had said he needed to be ready for the answers, and Harry thought he was. What Harry *really* wondered, though, was if he even had the right questions.

He parked his bike outside of the magic shop. He'd been inside the shop hundreds of times, but this time felt different. When he grabbed the doorknob, his hands were sweaty. He turned it, sure it would be locked. It wasn't. To Harry's surprise, the knob turned freely in his hand. Harry pushed the door open, and the little bell jingled over his head.

"Samson?" Harry asked as he stepped inside.

"Harry Moon, I presume," came Samson's voice from elsewhere in the store. "Would you kindly lock the door behind you?"

"Sure thing," Harry said. He turned and flipped the lock. It made a solid *thunk* noise. "Why was it unlocked?"

"I didn't want you to have to knock," Samson said, still hiding somewhere in the shop. "You're always welcome here."

95

"But it's six in the morning," Harry pointed out.

"That it is. But I had a feeling you'd be coming by. Call it a hunch."

With that, Samson came out of one of the aisles. He was putting up inventory, pushing a small cart filled with knickknacks and magical items.

"Is it okay that I'm here so early?" Harry asked.

"Yes. Like I said, you're always welcome here."

Samson pushed the inventory cart to the counter at the back. Harry followed him, realizing just how much the Sleepy Hollow Magic Shoppe felt like home to him.

"How can I help you?" Samson asked, taking a seat behind the counter.

Harry climbed on one of the stools on the other side of the counter. He leaned on the counter with his elbows. "I am going to be honest here," he said. "I have a question for you."

Samson smiled. "Have you ever not been honest? I suspect not. Ask away, friend."

Harry cleared his throat. "Okay . . . where have you been when you come back to the shop at five in the morning?"

Samson stopped smiling and wrinkled his brow. "Hmm. And how in the world would you know that? Have you been doing a little spying on your friend Samson?"

"No, no, no," Harry shook his head. "I took up Declan's paper route this week while he was at Disney World. Every morning, I saw you come back from somewhere. It was every morning at the same time while it was still kinda dark. You know, the first light thing. But I know it was you."

91

Samson cleared his throat and spoke with care. "It was. It was me. Every morning."

"But where were you?" Harry asked. "There is nothing open in Sleepy Hollow that early. I know you weren't out walking because I was biking around town delivering those papers, and I never saw you. Where were you?"

"Well, I don't know if you were supposed to see that just yet." Samson turned away from Harry, busying himself with the inventory. "Maybe that's for me to know and you to find out."

He wasn't saying it in a mean way. He sounded sort of like Rabbit when Rabbit spoke in weird little riddles. Harry almost felt like he was being tested in a way.

"That's why I'm here, Samson," he said. "To find out. Rabbit said to ask you and to *let go*. He said the answer might change me."

Samson turned back toward Harry and stared into his eyes for a moment. A little smile touched the corners of his mouth as he said, "Rabbit was right."

"So, where were you?" Harry asked.

"Rather than tell you, how about I *show* you?"

"Really? Awesome!"

"But not this very moment. Tomorrow morning, come by here at 4:30. Can you do that for me?"

"But I need to deliver the papers," Harry

said. "It's my last day."

"Oh, I think I can handle that," Samson said with a wink. "Just be here at 4:30. You and I will take a little trip. Sound good?"

Harry nodded enthusiastically. It *did* sound good. And even though he'd had a great week delivering Declan's papers, this secret he and Samson were sharing was easily the best part of the entire week.

99

Mary Moon sat on a bench along the edge of the Ladybug Trail playground, watching Harvest totter through a little plastic tunnel. The tunnel led to a yellow slide, which he had gone down roughly fifty times that afternoon. A few other kids were at the playground. From time to time, Harvest would join them. Most of the time, though, he preferred to stay by himself. Harvest was all about exploring, figuring out what his little body could do. What it *could* do was crawl through tunnels, make itty bitty sand castles, and go down the yellow slide. What it could not do was climb the monkey bars or lift his mother up on the see saw.

Mary spent some of her afternoons here at the Ladybug Trail playground with Harvest whenever her work schedule allowed. She was still dressed in her nurse's uniform, but that was fine with her. Harvest needed this time with her. Harry and Honey had their own friends they spent time with, and John would not be home for another hour.

Mary enjoyed this time with her younger son even though he seemed to be happier when she was on the bench and he was exploring things by himself. As she watched him climb the tiny little steps to the yellow ladder, she didn't realize that someone was walking her way. It was a man coming down Ladybug Trail directly toward her.

When she finally saw the man approaching, all she saw was a long purple robe and the golden crown on his head. That was more than enough for Mary to recognize the man.

"Samson," she said. "Well, hello there."

"Hi, Mary," Samson said. "Would you mind if I sat?"

"Help yourself," she said, scooting over on the bench to allow more room.

Samson sat down next to her and looked out at the playground. A wide smile spread across his face as he watched the children at play. "Mary, you've done a fantastic job raising your children. All three of them are quite special, I must say."

"Thank you," she said. She was never quite sure how to respond when Samson was around. She was especially taken off guard today given that she had spent a great deal of last night thinking about the odd conversation they'd had in the town square so many years ago.

"I was wondering if we might talk about Harry," Samson said.

"What about Harry?" she asked.

"Well, I would hope you trust me by now. I hope I have showed time and time again that I care a great deal about Harry. Not as much as you do, I'm sure. But still, I have a very special place in my heart for Harry."

"Yes, I know you do. Samson . . . is there something wrong?"

No," he said, still looking out at the children, Currently, Harvest was making a little mound of sand beneath the yellow slide.

"Then, what is it?"

"I believe the time has come for him to take a very important step. In order for him to become the fully realized hope that Sleepy Hollow will need one day, there's something he needs to do. This thing is quite safe, and I can walk him through it easily. But I need to borrow him quite early in the morning and share something special with him."

"What are you sharing with him?" she asked.

Samson thought about this for a moment before he answered. "I suppose you could say I am going to show him how to grow—how to tap into what is so special about him. And I will need to take him somewhere very close by in order to do that. Would you allow me to do this, Mary?"

It was Mary's turn to consider things now.

103

While she did trust Samson with Harry, things were, well, they were different now. Harry was older. In a few weeks, he would be in high school. He was no longer her little boy, but he was still something special.

Of course, Samson knew about that something special. In fact, Samson seemed to appreciate it and understand it better than Mary did. He'd been the one to tell her about it before she even had any idea.

That's why she finally nodded. "Yes, that would be fine," she said. "As long as you keep him safe and there is no danger."

"No, this is not dangerous at all. You have my word."

"Okay," she said. "When will this happen?"

"Tomorrow."

"But he has his paper route," Mary said.

"Yes, I know. I have thought about all of that, and I assure you, I have it all figured out."

Mary nodded once more. She could not explain why, but she felt safe with Samson sitting next to her. She felt that Harry would be safe with him. More than that, she was reminded of just how remarkable her oldest child was.

Beneath the slide, Harvest had knocked over his little sand pile and was starting on another one.

"Well," Samson said. "I'd best get back to work. Thank you, Mary. I'll take very good care of your son. And thank you for trusting me."

"Of course," she said.

Mary watched him get up and walk back the way he had come. His purple robe swished behind him as he waved and smiled to other passing mothers and their children.

While Samson had filled her with a sense of peace, she couldn't help but wonder where he might be taking Harry and what they would be doing.

He's growing up too fast, Mary thought. *How did Harry get so old so quickly?*

She was torn from her thoughts by a little hand patting her on the knee. Harvest had walked over and was asking to be picked up. He was probably getting hungry and was trying to tell her it was time to go.

With a smile, Mary picked him up and hugged him a little tighter than usual.

First Light and Second Thought

On Saturday morning, Harry started the paper route as usual. He arrived behind the office, attached the basket of papers to his handlebars, and set off. He delivered a few papers, keeping a close eye on the time. When the clock on his phone read 4:25, he forgot about delivering the papers and headed straight back toward the magic shop.

When he arrived, Samson was already standing behind the closed shop door. He gave Harry a wave and stepped out. He locked the door behind him and tucked the keys into his robe.

"Right on time," Samson said. "Now, I suppose the first thing we need to do is make sure your papers get delivered. What do you say?"

"Sure," Harry said, curious to see what tricks Samson had up his sleeves.

"Please hop off your bike," Samson said.

Harry did as he was asked while Samson pulled a wand from the inside of his robe. Samson flicked his wand at the pedals of Harry's bike. When he did, he said a little rhyme in the same way Harry did from time to time. Harry wondered if the words came to Samson in the same way they came to him—like someone had planted them like seeds in his head to sprout up at the right time.

Harry watched in wonder as Samson flicked the wand and said:
Be swift, be prompt,
be right on time!
Deliver these papers
for this friend of mine!

With that, the pedals on Harry's bike came to life. The bike popped a little wheelie and then started off down Magic Row by itself. As Harry watched, one paper came out of the basket and threw itself at Chillie Willies.

109

"Whoa," Harry said. "That's awesome."

"And efficient," Samson said.

In wonder, Harry watched as another paper flew from the basket and landed perfectly upon the door mat of the Ghost Busters store.

"Now, along we go," said Samson.

"Where are we going?"

"It doesn't matter where we are going," said Samson. "It matters when we arrive."

"I have no idea what you just said," Harry replied.

Samson smiled in the soft darkness of the morning. "I know, my young friend. Just come along."

110

In the murk of early morning, they made their way down the lighted street and turned off into the Sleepy Hollow forest and up through the woods and hills overlooking the sleeping town. Harry puffed a little keeping up with Samson, almost stumbling a few times over branches Samson deftly stepped over. Harry came through these same woods every now and again with his friends, sometimes pretending to be on great quests and sometimes just talking about guy stuff. He had a pretty good idea of where they were, especially when they crossed the little wooden bridge that carried them over a stream.

They were cutting around the eastern side of town, the woods taking them behind Sleepy Hollow High and winding toward Moon Lake. But before Moon Lake, Harry knew, was Wonder Wood Road. In fact, Wonder Wood Road led out to Moon Lake after a few miles.

"Are we going to Moon Lake?" Harry asked. He certainly hoped not. That would be a very long walk.

"No. And Harry, please, no questions for now. Let's just enjoy the silence."

Harry obeyed and continued to follow Samson. They walked for twenty minutes, and after a healthy trek, they emerged into a clearing that sat above the still dark of Sleepy Hollow. Harry's eyes darted back and forth, looking for his own home. There it was, barely lighted under the street lamps. It was hardly recognizable in the unusual light of the early morning.

Down below the clearing, there was a winding stretch of blacktop surrounded by trees. *Wonder*

Wood Road, Harry thought.

More than that, Harry noticed a familiar event taking place along the horizon. First light was approaching, but it seemed different today. In realizing this, he started to feel the sensation that had brought tears to his eyes for a while on Thursday morning.

"It's amazing how everything looks so different this early," Harry said. "This strange light . . . it is different every morning."

"That's because there are no two days that are alike. Every first light will as different as the days are. You see things you don't normally see in full light."

"So, is this why you come out here? For first light?"

Samson shook his head. "Partially. But it's what comes along with it that brings me here."

Harry looked around. "What's that?"

Samson put his finger up to his lips. "Shhh. What do you hear?"

Harry looked around and listened. He could see first light inking its way into the world, and he was very aware of that warm, flushed feeling. But the world was absolutely silent.

"I don't hear anything. What am I supposed

to hear?"

Samson smiled and raised a finger. His eyes were closed, and a smile had come to his face. "That. Right there."

"What?" Harry asked, starting to get a little flustered.

"Nothing."

"How can I hear nothing? How can I hear something when nothing is there? I don't get it!"

Samson turned toward Harry. He had the look of a teacher that was about to lay down some serious lessons. "What did Rabbit tell you to do when you asked me where I am every morning?" Samson asked.

"He said to 'let go,'" Harry said.

"So, let go. When I ask you what you hear and you hear nothing, what is left to hear? What is *behind* the nothing?"

Harry stood in the silence. "All I hear is my own voice in my head."

Samson smiled. "Then it's time to introduce yourself. I don't believe the two of you have ever met."

Harry started to speak, and Samson held up a finger.

"Shhh," Samson whispered. "Listen. Not to the first voice you hear in your head—not the first thought. Wait for the second thought. Be quiet for a moment. You will hear it. Your second thought is your doorway to the Deep Magic. Rarely is the first thing that comes to mind the wise thought. Our first thought is usually wrong. It's born from instinct. The wisdom we look for is found in second thought, which is deeper than instinct."

Samson put his hand on Harry's shoulder. "It's the second thought we listen for, Harry. And we can only find it in the quiet. The Deep Magic is found in the quiet."

Harry stood alone in the first light. He listened. He bowed his head toward the ground and closed his eyes and let the quiet wrap itself around him. Once he could focus on the something behind the nothing, it started to become easier.

The voice in his head seemed to split up and become two and then three and then four. He squeezed his eyes tight, and the voices grew from soft to loud and came together in a single voice like the sound from a choir. His skin started tingling. The feeling of first light bloomed inside of him. His heart felt like it was floating, and every muscle beneath his skin seemed to buzz with a very gentle electricity.

With his eyes still closed, Harry dropped to his knees and placed his hands on the dewy ground and gripped the grass, greeting each blade as they wrapped themselves around his fingers. The sound in his head was no longer a sound, but a song that drifted through every inch of his magician's body. He leaned forward until the top of his head settled on the ground, and he felt the dirt breathing and the trees speaking. And in the first light of the morning, Harry Moon, for the first time in his young life, had a second thought.

After a bit of time that he did not know, Harry gasped and straightened up and opened his eyes. He brushed the back of his hand across his cheek and found it wet.

"Have I been crying?" he asked Samson.

Samson got down on one knee and looked into the glistening eyes of his friend, the corners of his own eyes crinkling.

117

"Welcome. Welcome to the Deep Magic, Harry Moon."

118

A FOREVER FIGHT

They stood there for a moment, looking down onto the town. It looked like someone had pulled a large black canvas over everything and only the shapes remained. The streetlights were as small as little fireflies from where they stood.

Harry looked down at it, feeling strange. He thought he would be pumped and full of energy to have finally touched the Deep Magic. Instead, though, he felt worn out. He also felt something else—a word that escaped him for a while, but he finally managed to figure it out. He felt humbled.

"This is the Deep Magic?" Harry asked.

"It's part of it, yes," Samson said. "But it's so much more than just a feeling. Once you have felt it, you can sort of tap into it. It becomes something that you can rely on. Something that becomes a part of you without you even knowing it."

Harry thought he understood. He still focused on the noise behind the nothing, the perfect stillness that sounded almost like a choir. The second thought.

"So, this is where you come every morning?" Harry asked.

"Almost every morning, yes," Samson said.

"How long have you been coming here?"

Samson smiled as they neared the little wooden bridge that carried them across a meandering stream. "Long enough."

"Does it have to be this spot?" Harry asked. "Is there something about this clearing or Wonder Wood Road?"

"I believe so," Samson said. "But I'm sure there are other areas in town where one might get a glimpse of a perfect first light and, more importantly, experience second thought. But I know this is a place of power for sure. I sense you are a little confused about this?"

"Well, not confused. Not really. It's just that . . . I felt something on Wonder Wood Road earlier this week. It was a really welcoming sort of feeling. I felt it in my heart, and I almost cried. It made me want to keep riding down Wonder Wood Road. But when I started down that way, I heard something else. A voice in my head sort of. It told me—"

"I bet it said 'Stop. Turn back.' Right?"

"That's right," Harry said, shocked that Samson seemed to have read his mind. "How did you know that?"

"Because I have heard it, too," Samson said. "See, around the time of first light, this part of the town can be quite powerful. The thing that you and I just experienced together—first light and the second thought—has an opposite. And they both reside here in Sleepy Hollow. It just so happens that because of Mayor Kligore's curse, the opposite is usually stronger."

"You mean evil?" Harry asked.

"Some might call it that," Samson said. "You're a smart and insightful boy, Harry. I take it you have an understanding of how the world we live in is a broken world, correct?"

"Yes."

"Well, it's no different here in Sleepy Hollow. We're trapped in time, always stuck in a state of

Halloween. And until that curse is broken, the darkness is going to be stronger than it should be. Do you understand?"

"I think so."

"Those two feelings—the need to go deeper down Wonder Wood Road and the voice telling you to stop—they both exist out here. And perhaps other areas in town."

"Where does that power come from?" Harry asked.

"It comes from the Place of Beginnings," Samson said. "In the same way you and I can experience second thought, Mayor Kligore and those who serve him have their own powers. All of that power is drawn from the Place of Beginnings. It provides the magic for both sides. It's where our Deep Magic comes from, but it's also where the mayor goes to power his dark magic. The Place of Beginnings is the source for all."

"Beginnings?" Harry asked. "What was there

before the Place of Beginnings?"

Samson smiled. "Never was there such a thing." He straightened his robes with a brush of his hands.

"Where did the Place of Beginnings come from?" Harry asked.

"Enough of the questions, my dear friend. Although, I suppose I expected as much. No worries, like most answers, it is best to show you. But you must be very quiet and especially careful. Can you do that?"

"Yes," Harry said, still rocked by having experienced second thought and felt first light.

Samson walked to the edge of the clearing and into another strip of forest. This forest was much thinner; as soon as they stepped into it, Harry could see another clearing just beyond it. Only this clearing looked odd. First light was still revealing itself, but it seemed stronger here. Thursday, Harry had thought first light made the sky seem alive. Now, looking at it in the clearing beyond the trees, he thought he could actually see the sky breathing.

"Slowly," Samson said. He placed a hand on Harry's shoulder to slow him.

They came to the edge of the forest, and Harry found himself looking down a slight hill. First light was still visible, but he could sense that dawn would overtake it very soon. Harry looked down the hill and took a huge step back. His eyes went wide with fear.

"Samson, what is this?"

Samson did not answer. He simply let Harry look. And Harry did not like what he saw.

Down at the bottom of the hill was what looked like a thin tear in the sky. Wavering lines of misty light seeped out of it almost as if it were hiding a very small sun. It was this effect that had made Harry think the sky might be breathing. That's exactly what it looked like. The faint light spilled out of the tear but quickly curled back in.

As if this was not crazy enough, there were several figures standing down at the bottom of the hill. Thanks to the soft light glowing from the tear in the sky, Harry could see the figures perfectly clearly.

"That's Mayor Kligore!" Harry hissed from the edge of the forest.

"Indeed," Samson said.

But that wasn't all. Harry saw all sorts of other figures down there. He saw Cherry Tomato, Marcus Kligore, Oink, Ug, and three robed figures that he assumed were members of the Quiet Ones. They were all standing still and not speaking. They seemed to be looking directly into the tear.

"What are they doing?" Harry asked.

"The same thing you and I were just doing. Only the opposite, like I said."

"I don't understand."

"First light is very powerful," Samson said. "That tear you see in the sky down there is the Place of Beginnings I mentioned. That's where the power to receive second thought and the Deep Magic comes from."

"Then what good would it do Mayor Kligore and his dumb friends?" Harry asked.

"He draws his power from it too," Samson explained. Seeing that Harry was clearly confused, he went on as best he could. "You see, Harry, the light and the dark have always been in a fight—a forever fight, if you will. That is especially true here in Sleepy Hollow. Remember our broken world, Harry. It was not always like this. Everything was made by the Great Magician. But then the world changed. The world was broken. Some things became very bad. But that does not change the fact that it still all rests under the hands of the Great Magician. The Place of Beginnings down there is of the Great Magician and, therefore, is a good thing. But because we live in a broken world, Kligore is also able to tap into it. Something like

127

first light can't be hidden from everyone. Sadly, though, Mayor Kligore has chosen to exploit the power within the Place of Beginnings."

"I'm sorry," Harry said. "I still don't get it."

"Think of it this way," Samson said. "When the world became broken, it affected not only people, but the whole world too. The earth itself wants things fixed. It *groans* for things to be back to the way they were. The Great Magician is allowing us to use for good something Kligore has chosen to use for evil."

"This forever fight. Will it happen here?" Harry asked.

"It's happening here right now," Samson said. "And everywhere else. But I do think that one day you will be a big part in putting an end to that fight here in Sleepy Hollow."

Harry thought about all of this and frowned, a little confused. "So . . . when I felt second thought in that clearing, was I getting it from the Place of Beginnings?"

"Yes," Samson nodded. "Not all answers are ever to be known, but what you say is true. Never will you breathe more deeply the Deep Magic than at the Place of Beginnings."

"I guess the feeling I had on Wonder Wood Road when I was delivering papers was sort of like second thought," Harry said. "It was the Deep Magic reaching out from the Place of Beginnings, wanting me to see it. But the voice telling me to turn back was the dark magic wanting to keep me away."

"Exactly. You've got it figured out now."

"So now that I have felt the Deep Magic, you say it's a part of me now?"

"Yes, indeed."

"So how do I—"

But as Harry was about to ask his question, the first rays of sunlight appeared over the horizon. At the same moment, the tear in the sky grew into nothing more than mist and then disappeared completely.

It was all quite majestic and happened so quickly that Harry took a step back. When he did, he backed right into a tree. He lost his footing and fell on his backside. When he hit the ground, there wasn't too much noise, but there was apparently just enough to be heard.

Down at the bottom of the hill, every figure that had been staring at the horizon turned and looked in their direction.

"Ah, crud," Harry said.

"Looks like we've been found out," Samson said.

Right away, the three Quiet Ones started up the hill toward them. Harry noticed right away that they floated along the hill, coming along like growing shadows. He saw no feet pushing them forward at all, and they were moving very fast. Behind them, Mayor Kligore pointed a very angry-looking finger in Harry's direction.

"Harry Moon!" he shouted. "What are you doing here? You and your pathetic magician friend have no business here!"

Harry started to run off, but Samson once again placed a calming hand on his shoulder. "Why are you running?" he asked.

"Because there's no telling what Kligore will do to me after seeing this!"

"Oh, no doubt," Samson said, looking down the hill. The Quiet Ones were very close now. They'd be in the forest in less than ten seconds.

131

"You've apparently forgotten," Samson said, "that I always travel with a means of transportation."

With that, Samson expertly removed his robe. He tossed it into the air, flicked his wand at it, and it straightened out into a perfectly square shape before it hit the ground. In fact, it did not hit the ground at all. It hovered in the air, waiting for its riders.

"Impenetrable!" Harry exclaimed.

"Ah, so you *do* remember!"

Of course, Harry remembered. He'd had the chance to ride Samson's magic carpet of a robe on one other occasion, and it had been amazing. Now, however, Impenetrable might very well end up saving his life.

Together, Samson and Harry stepped on

and took a seat. Just as Impenetrable raised itself into the air, the three Quiet Ones entered the forest behind them. Harry turned to look and saw those red eyes glowing like hot coals from within their pitch-black hood.

"Get us out of here, Samson!"

"You heard the young man, Impenetrable," Samson said. "To speed!"

Impenetrable was happy to oblige. It continued to raise up into the trees, nearing the treetops, and then rocketed forward.

133

Only Harry did not go with it.

Just as the magic carpet catapulted forward, Harry felt something tug at the back of his shirt. Suddenly, Impenetrable was no longer beneath him; there was only open sky and treetops.

But then he *was* moving, only not with Samson. One of the Quiet Ones had snatched him from Impenetrable and was now carrying him out of the forest. They were getting lower and lower to the ground, and beneath Harry's feet, Mayor Kligore was staring up at him with an evil smile on his face.

Outnumbered

The Quiet One was not gentle when it released Harry. It dropped Harry ten feet or so to the ground. Harry landed on his feet but then went pitching forward with an incredible pain in his left ankle. He rolled a few feet farther down the hill before stopping himself with his hands. A few feet up the hill, Mayor Kligore, Cherry Tomato, Oink, Ug, and Marcus all roared with laughter.

"You've got some nerve," Mayor Kligore said. "You've meddled in my affairs before, but this is a very private matter. And here you are, all alone. What do you think I should do with him, crew?"

"End him," Marcus said.

"Hang him upside down by his shoelaces from a tree," Oink suggested.

"Pull out each of his fingernails," Cherry Tomato offered.

The Quiet Ones remained silent. But their silence was just as bad as any of the suggestions that had been made.

Harry was ashamed of it, but he found himself wanting to beg and plead his way out of the situation. He knew there was no way out of this. Maybe if he could make some sort of offer to the mayor he could get out of this mostly unharmed.

No, Harry thought. *That's cowardly. And it was also the first thought that came to me. It was my first thought, not second thought.*

Harry said nothing to his captors. Instead, he closed his eyes for a moment. Even though first light was no longer visible in the sky, he could feel its echoes. More than that, he could feel the Deep Magic, lurking within him like some big, beautiful fish beneath the surface of an endless ocean.

131

And then second thought came to him. It was a scary thought, but he accepted it with a bravery he had never before experienced.

Harry slowly got to his feet and reached around into his backpack. When he withdrew his wand, the looks on the faces of the bullies in front of him were amused. They'd all thought he'd just chicken out because he was so outnumbered.

"Are you kidding me?" Mayor Kligore asked. "Little Harry Moon against all of us? Very well then. I've waited for this day for a very long time and I—"

"ABRACADABRA!"

Harry flicked his wand and made a tiny circular motion. Mayor Kligore was fast enough to avoid it, raising his arm and blocking it with a spell of his own. But Harry's spell bounced from the mayor and struck Ug. The minion went flying backward and rolling down the hill, his little rat-like tail flipping over and over.

Marcus was advancing on him now. Harry was pretty sure Marcus wasn't very talented in terms of magic, but that didn't matter. The fists he was making at his sides were scary enough. Harry had bested Marcus before, but something was different now. Now, Harry was severely outnumbered, and the silence of the hillside clearing seemed to be pressing in around him.

Harry raised his wand and was about to

shout a spell at Marcus when he caught sight of one of the Quiet Ones closing in on his right. Having to decide if he'd rather be slugged by Marcus or grabbed by a Quiet One, Harry redirected his wand at the Quiet One.

For a second, he could do nothing. His mouth could not form words, and his arm could not move his wand. He was staring into those red eyes and felt paralyzed with fear. There seemed to be nothing else behind the hood, just an impossible gloom.

139

He pushed past his fear. It dropped out of his mind and heart and was replaced by a sense of calm—the same overwhelming feeling he'd felt in the clearing with Samson several minutes ago.

Second thought. The Deep Magic.

Feeling the Deep Magic spiral through him, Harry wasn't scared at all. He was nearly confident as the shouted "ABRACADABRA!"

At once, the black cloak of the Quiet One

folded in on itself. This revealed that there was no real body beneath the cloak, just a sort of mist. The cloak billowed backward, sending the Quiet One tumbling to the ground in a bundle of dark cloth and long, thin arms.

Harry had no time to enjoy this small victory, though. Marcus was suddenly in front of him. He gave Harry an enormous shove that sent Harry to the ground. The wind went whooshing out of him, and his wand went tumbling out of reach.

140

"That's enough of that nonsense, Moon Man," Marcus said. "Dad, permission to pound him?"

Mayor Kligore joined his son. That evil smile was still on his face. Harry looked around and saw that they were surrounding him. Even Ug had rejoined them. He looked a little embarrassed to have been sent tumbling down the hill.

"Permission granted," the mayor said. "But don't break anything. A hospital visit could

cause problems for We Drive By Night. But by all means, make it hurt."

Marcus stepped forward. Without his wand, Harry had no idea what to do. He knew there was no way he could take Marcus in a fight. And even if he managed to get away from Marcus, there were three Quiet Ones, the mayor, Cherry Tomato, Ug, and Oink to contend with.

Marcus smiled down at Harry and drew his arm back. Harry cringed, waiting for the punch to fall.

Instead, he heard a huge gust of air, followed by a scream from Mayor Kligore.

Harry looked to his left and saw Samson riding Impenetrable through the trees. The magic carpet was like a speeding bullet, so fast that Harry could see blurs of color along its side. Impenetrable came whizzing by, low to the ground and with ferocious speed. Cherry Tomato and Oink had to jump out of the way to avoid being hit.

Samson reached down and grabbed Harry as he passed by. In a single dizzying motion, Samson had Harry sitting on the back of Impenetrable. Harry turned and looked back at the ground as Impenetrable made a huge U-turn in the air as it rose up. Cherry Tomato was getting to her feet. Marcus was looking up at them as if he still had no clue what was happening. Mayor Kligore was shaking his fists at the sky and letting out a yell of defeat.

"Thanks, Samson," Harry said.

"No problem. I would have been here sooner, but it's rather hard to make a turn on Impenetrable when all of these trees are in the way."

They were rocketing through the trees now, heading back toward the first clearing Samson had brought him to. They were moving so fast that it was like being on a roller coaster. Trees whizzed by, some passing dangerously close. They reached the clearing, but Samson guided Impenetrable into the Sleepy Hollow woods where even more trees went by in blinding flashes. Samson did not bring the magic carpet to a stop until they were nearly on Magic Row.

143

"Harry, you did well back there," Samson said. "You stood up for yourself. You did not buckle under pressure."

"I felt the Deep Magic," Harry said. "I used second thought."

Samson smiled and ruffled Harry's hair.

"You're a natural, kiddo."

They walked the rest of the way through the forest and came out into Magic Row. Harry checked his phone and saw that it was 5:42. Morning sunlight had started to paint the sidewalks and buildings, but the town was mostly quiet. It was weird, but Harry thought the silence of a Saturday morning sounded different than the other days of the week.

"So, the Place of Beginnings goes away when first light disappears?" Harry asked.

"Yes," Samson said as they started down the sidewalk. "I believe first light and the Deep Magic together provide a very special access for us on earth. When first light passes so does direct access to the Place of Beginnings."

Harry nodded. He was pretty sure he understood, but it was a lot to think about. It made his brain feel heavy and tired.

"You have time to figure it out, Harry," Samson said. "But the Deep Magic is a part of

you now. Some things will just come to you. Certain things will seem clearer now. Of course, if you need help along the way . . . "

"I'll come to you," Harry said.

"Exactly."

Their shadows started to appear alongside them as they made their way back to the Sleepy Hollow Magic Shoppe. The shadow of a young boy and an older man followed their matching figures, coming together for just a moment as they rounded the curb.

145

✦

Harry's bike was waiting for him, propped against the side of the Magic Shoppe. The newspaper basket was still attached to his handlebars, but it was completely empty. Whatever enchantment Samson had cast upon it had successfully delivered the papers. Feeling a little sluggish but, at the same time, incredibly wired, Harry hopped on the bike. Samson unlocked the shop door and stepped inside.

Before closing the door, Samson looked out at Harry. "Having the Deep Magic inside of you is a very special thing, Harry. Treasure it, and always seek it when you are uncertain about something. One of these days, you'll find that it has become such a part of you that you almost take it for granted. But don't let that happen, Harry."

"I won't."

"Right, then. You have a good weekend, Harry."

"You, too."

With that, Samson closed his door and set the lock with a wave through the glass to Harry. Harry headed down Magic Row, angling over toward Main Street to return the empty newspaper basket. When he made it to the parking lot in the back, he saw Mildred Middlemarch getting out of her car.

"Hi, Harry," she said. "Did you have a good morning?"

He smiled and nodded. *You don't know the half of it,* he thought.

"I did," he said, handing her the empty newspaper basket.

"It was so nice to work with you," she said. "We didn't have a single complaint all week! If you ever want some sort of job with the newspaper, let me know. I'll see what I can do."

"Gee, thanks, Mrs. Middlemarch," Harry said. Then, after some thought, Harry added, "Can I ask you something?"

"Of course."

"Are you happy with your job? Do you ever, I don't know . . . do you ever feel freaked out to be working with Mayor Kligore and those Quite Ones?"

She shrugged. "It's the hand I've been dealt."

She said nothing else about it as she walked in through the back door. Harry thought her answer was one of the saddest things he'd ever heard. But he then thought about the Place of Beginnings out there on the other side of Wonder Wood Road and how Samson had said that all things serve the Great Magician—even things that might seem dark and hopeless.

He hoped Mrs. Middlemarch was being treated fairly. But he knew there was nothing he could do about it if she wasn't. Not yet, anyway.

But Samson had hinted at the fact that there would be a day where Harry might play a big part in helping the entire town. It was a scary thought, and the idea of the responsibility weighed on him like stones on his back. But, if it might help to one day free Sleepy Hollow residents like Mrs. Middlemarch and all others that had no choice but to accept the hand they'd been dealt, then the weight was worth it.

With that sense of duty in his heart, Harry pedaled back home. He suddenly wanted to be with his family.

. . . AND ALL I GOT WAS THIS LOUSY SHIRT

O n Sunday afternoon, Harry was headed home for dinner when he heard another bicycle approaching from behind him. He was halfway down Nightingale Lane when he stopped and turned to see who was coming. It wasn't dark yet, but the gathering dusk was just gray enough to have caused the streetlights to come on.

It was Declan, speeding up to close the distance between them. A plastic bag was swaying from his handlebars. When he pulled up next to Harry, he hit his brakes and placed a tire burn on the sidewalk. Both boys grinned at the mark for a while before greeting one another.

"Did you have a good trip?" Harry asked.

"Oh man, it was the best! Dad said he may have to go back next year. I can't wait."

"Sounds awesome," Harry said.

Declan handed Harry a plastic bag. Harry peeked inside and saw two T-shirts. "Thanks, man. You really didn't have to, though. I had a lot of fun with the paper route."

And learned quite a few things about Sleepy Hollow too, Harry thought but did not say.

"Yeah," Declan said. "You know, it's actually my favorite part of summer. It's the biggest reason I'm going to be bummed when school starts back. Hey, did you see what I was talking about? How the town is like this whole other place when it's so early?"

"I sure did. Oh, and hey! I met an older man out on Scarlett Letter Lake."

"In a rowboat, right? Yeah, that's Mr. Cod. He'd pretty cool. He's got some pretty crazy ideas, though. He goes out into the middle of the lake just about every morning and just sits."

151

"I think he enjoys the silence," Harry said. But really, Harry had done a lot of thinking about that old man. He wondered if Mr. Cod had got a small taste of what first light was really about and went out there time and time again hoping for some sort of understanding.

"And did you find out what I was talking about with the whole first light thing?"

Harry tried biting back a grin but couldn't

help it. "Oh yeah," he said. "Look, man, I had a blast. Thanks so much for thinking of me to cover for you."

"No problem. Anyway, I just wanted to give you these shirts. Thanks again. I better get home for dinner."

"Same here," Harry said. "See you tomorrow?"

152 "For sure."

Harry watched as Declan headed back down the street. It was good to have his friend back, but Harry was a little bummed that he didn't have the paper route anymore. He wondered if Declan might allow him to ride along with him on a few mornings before school started back.

Harry continued home, parking his bike and heading into the kitchen. His mom had made one of her thin pizzas. It made the house smell amazing. Harvest was coloring a piece of paper on the kitchen floor. Honey was in the living room, organizing all the weird things she kept in her turtle backpack. His dad was helping his mom by getting the organic toppings ready for the pizza. It was a typical Sunday afternoon, but it seemed clearer to Harry somehow. He saw in that moment how blessed he was to have such a family. He'd always known it, but now, it seemed to thrum inside of him.

The Deep Magic, Harry thought. *Is that what Samson meant about it becoming a part of me?*

If so, Harry thought it was pretty awesome.

He dashed upstairs to wash his hands and take his shoes off. As he kicked his sneakers across the room, he dumped the two T-shirts out of the plastic bag. Declan had picked some pretty sweet ones. He figured he'd wear one tomorrow. Sure, he had the Deep Magic now and felt a little wiser, but he still had no issues rocking a *Star Wars* tee.

Just before he headed back down to the kitchen, Rabbit hopped onto his bed. He glanced

at Harry with a smile, tilting his head. His ears flopped over comically.

"Harry, I must say, you look different."

Harry smiled and said, "I *feel* different."

"I take it you got the answers you were looking for?"

"Most of them," Harry said. "But . . . Rabbit?

Be honest with me. You already knew the answers, didn't you?"

"Maybe," Rabbit said. "But there are some things you just need to learn on your own. All the explaining in the world from a rabbit is nothing compared to an actual experience."

"So, you know about the Place of Beginnings?"

"I do. And I think you will too. Because there's something special inside of you, isn't there?"

"The Deep Magic."

Rabbit nodded. He then hopped down from the bed and went over to Harry. Rabbit nuzzled against Harry's leg for a moment and then looked up at him. When Harry looked into Rabbit's eyes, he was overcome with a feeling he got from time to time—a feeling that Rabbit was much more than a Rabbit. Harry could see something majestic sparkling in those dark eyes.

"I'm proud of you, Harry."

"Thanks," Harry said, giving Rabbit a scratch between the ears.

A moment passed between them. Harry thought he might cry, and not in some mysterious way caused by the Deep Magic or whatever had passed through him during the first time he'd truly experienced first light. No, these were plain, old happy tears.

Maybe it was the Deep Magic that was making him more aware of simple things. In that moment, what Harry realized was this: from great friends, to a loving family, to a wondrous sidekick like Rabbit, Harry was indeed truly blessed.

And that was perhaps the most magical thing of all.

MARK ANDREW POE

Harry Moon author Mark Andrew Poe never thought about being a children's writer growing up. His dream was to love and care for animals, specifically his friends in the rabbit community.

Along the way, Mark became successful in all sorts of interesting careers. He entered the print and publishing world as a young man, and his company did really, really well.

Mark became a popular and nationally sought-after health care advocate for the care and well-being of rabbits.

Years ago, Mark came up with the idea of a story about a young man with a special connection to a world of magic, all revealed through a remarkable rabbit friend. Mark worked on his idea for several years before building a collaborative creative team to help bring his idea to life. And Harry Moon was born.

In 2014, Mark began a multi-book print series project intended to launch *The Adventures of Harry Moon* into the youth marketplace as a hero defined by a love for a magic where love and 'DO NO EVIL' live. Today, Mark continues to work on the many stories of Harry Moon. He lives in suburban Chicago with his wife and his twenty-five rabbits.

Fantalk With Harry!

Q: WHAT DO YOU HOPE FANS LEARN OR TAKE AWAY FROM YOUR STORIES, HARRY?

A: I dunno. I guess that kids should be confident in themselves and not let themselves get bullied around and how important good friends are.

Q: YOU TALK ABOUT BEING BULLIED BY TITUS IN YOUR MIDDLE SCHOOL. WHAT DO YOU HOPE KIDS LEARN FROM YOU ABOUT HOW TO DEAL WITH A BULLY LIKE TITUS?

A. It's not fun to be bullied. It's actually scary. Sometimes the only thing you can do is tell somebody that it is happening because sometimes it, like, wrecks your life. For me, I decided that I would try and make the bully my friend by being kind to him rather than being afraid. For me, it worked. It doesn't always work. Believe me, I know.

Q. YOU SHARE WITH KIDS YOUR LOVE OF MAGIC. HOW DID YOU DEVELOP THAT LOVE? HOW DID YOU LEARN TO DO MAGIC TRICKS?

A. It wasn't that I loved magic, but I loved being able to do things that surprised people. I liked hearing them say, "How did he do that?!" Along the way I discovered there was the play magic and that there was "real, deep magic." That is when everything changed for me. Samson taught me that.

Q. WHAT WAS YOUR FIRST IMPRESSION OF HIM? WHAT DID YOU LEARN FROM HIM?

A. My first impression of Samson was that he was a very old, goofy guy. Not many adults pay attention to you when you are a kid. I liked him almost right away. He taught me the deep magic, not to be afraid of the dark, and the power of good mischief.

163

Q: YOU AND YOUR MOM CAN TALK ABOUT ANYTHING. EVEN WHEN YOU DON'T AGREE WITH ONE ANOTHER, YOU TWO LOVE EACH OTHER. HOW DOES YOUR FAMILY MAKE YOU FEEL LOVED EVEN WHEN YOU ARE HAVING A DISAGREEMENT?

A: I think mainly by not yelling and talking to me like a person and letting me have an opinion that is different than theirs. When I am at my friends' houses, I am always surprised how they are treated like babies by their parents and yelled at all the time. I would hate that.

Q. YOU KNOW YOUR MOM IS NOT CRAZY ABOUT
MAGIC AND TELLS YOU TO BE CAREFUL. WHY
IS YOUR MOM NOT CRAZY ABOUT MAGIC?

A. Probably because she doesn't understand it. I think she is also afraid that magic may be dangerous for me. Of course, it's the opposite.

Q. YOU AND YOUR MOM HAVE HAD DISCUSSIONS ABOUT "TRUE POWER" AND WHERE IT COMES FROM. CAN YOU EXPLAIN TO THE KIDS WHAT "REAL" POWER IS AND WHERE IT COMES FROM?

A. Of course not. No one really understands. It's a mystery. I just know that it comes from a special place of goodness.

Q. Samson from the magic store gave you a special rabbit. He's more than a pet. Can you tell readers what it means to have Rabbit, who has become your friend?

A. It means that I am never alone and that I have a friend that is always smarter than me and that will help me if I let him. It's not easy having a friend like Rabbit. It means that I have to admit I might be wrong a lot. A whole lot.

165

Q. I SAW THAT YOUR FRIEND RABBIT SAID TO YOU, "HAVING A FRIEND LIKE ME HAS CONSEQUENCES." WHAT DOES HE MEAN BY THAT?

A. Well, if you had a friend like Rabbit, you wouldn't ask that question.

Q. WHAT WAS YOUR FAVORITE STORY YOU SHARED WITH READERS IN YOUR BOOKS, HARRY?

A. I think the first time Sarah kissed me. Yikes.

Q. WHICH STORY WAS THE HARDEST FOR YOU TO SHARE? WHY? WHAT DO YOU HOPE KIDS TAKE AWAY AS YOU SHARE IT?

A. That's easy. Its my relationship with my parents. You can read it all in the stories. Sometimes kids make fun that I am so close to my mom and dad. When you are in eighth grade, its cooler sometimes to put your parents down and stuff. So, its kinda embarrassing that we get along, even though we argue sometimes. I guess I would want kids to know that their parents may be cooler than they think.

Q. WHAT KEEPS YOU NORMAL IN THE MIDDLE OF THE CRAZINESS OF SLEEPY HOLLOW? IN THE MIDDLE OF ALL THAT STRESS AND GOOFINESS GOING THROUGH MIDDLE SCHOOL?

A. Life in eighth grade and living in Sleepy Hollow can drive you crazy. Rabbit keeps reminding me to keep my head up and to look behind everything to understand what is really going on. He also reminds me that a lot of kids can be mean and to remember that a lot of them are really hurting themselves. And, of course, good mischief.

Q: **WHAT THREE THINGS ARE YOU MOST THANKFUL FOR IN LIFE?**

A: My family, Samson, and Rabbit. And, of course, Sarah.

167

Q. CAN YOU GIVE US A SNEAK PEEK INTO WHAT
ADVENTURES YOU'LL SHARE WITH KIDS IN
YOUR NEXT BOOK?

A. I think the Sleepy Hollow story is just going
to keep rolling out. There are so many. I will
just say this: Oink is going to get his.

Q. WHAT'S THE BEST ADVICE YOUR PARENTS OR
CLOSE FRIENDS HAVE GIVEN YOU?

A. That is easy. It's from Rabbit:

DO NO EVIL.

HARRY MOON'S
DNA

Helps his fellow schoolmates
Makes friends with those who had once been his enemies
Respects nature
Honors his body
Does not categorize people too quickly
Seeks wisdom from adults
Guides the young
Controls his passions
Is curious
Understands that life will have trouble and accepts it
And, of course, loves his mom!

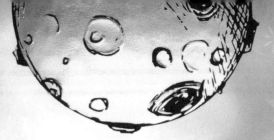

COMING SOON!
MORE MAGICAL ADVENTURES

POSTER INSIDE!

HARRY MOON

PROFESSOR EINSTONE

MARK ANDREW POE

HARRY MOON

TICKLISH

POSTER INSIDE!

MARK ANDREW POE

POSTER INSIDE!

HARRY MOON

HALLOWEEN NIGHTMARES

MARK ANDREW POE

POSTER INSIDE!

HARRY MOON

HARRY'S CHRISTMAS CAROL

MARK ANDREW POE

Honey Moon's
DNA

Builds friendships that matter
Goes where she is needed
Helps fellow classmates
Speaks her mind
Honors her body
Does not categorize others
Loves to have a blast
Seeks wisdom from adults
Desires to be brave
Sparkles away
And, of course, loves her mom

POSTER INSIDE!

HONEY MOON

SKELETONS IN THE CLOSET

SOFI BENITEZ

POSTER INSIDE!

HONEY MOON

DOG DAZE

SOFI BENITEZ

POSTER INSIDE!

HONEY MOON

SCARY LITTLE CHRISTMAS

SOFI BENITEZ

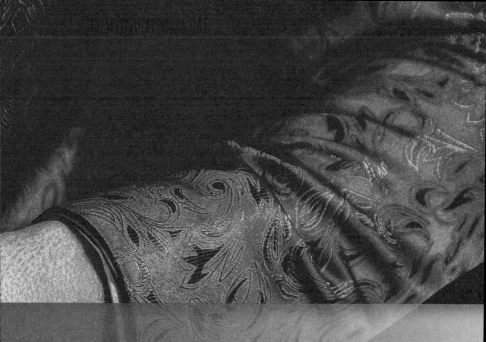

Splendiferous (adj): Absolutely fantastic

There was an old man who slept on the side of the road. His skin was so shiny that his bones showed through. His feet were worn. His soles were as thin as leaves. His skull was laced with blue veins that throbbed when his heart beat.

Around his waist, the old man wore a little rag. The rag also ran up past his belly button and over the shoulder. The rag was both a loin cloth, like Tarzan wore, and a sash, like a decorated king.

But this rag was not always this way.

When the man was about to be born, his poor parents looked out the window. They saw stars gathered like fireflies at the windowsill. The stars never took a form but to shimmer and sparkle in the night sky. The mother could hear the stars sing, "Watch over your baby and his splendiferous coat."

As the little boy grew, so did the coat. It grew longer and longer, keeping up with the stride of the boys' growing legs. When the boy became a man, strong and handsome, the splendiferous coat fit him perfectly.

When the young man needed rest, the coat covered him from head-to-toe. When he needed food, he reached into the pockets of the coat and food was there for him.

When he was lonely, he curled up in his

splendiferous garment, and he felt warm and cozy and strong. He did not feel alone at all.

The young man traveled the road, and he had many adventures. He slayed dragons. He saved maidens. He rescued the vulnerable. Through the years, the splendiferous coat served him well.

Wherever he traveled, the man washed the coat in the rivers and the streams so the coat could be fresh and clean again.

One night, the man fought a wolf in the woods. The man escaped the wolf but the beast left a rip at the back of the coat that could never be mended. As the years passed, the beautiful coat began to wear. There was wear on the back due to the fight with the wolf. There was wear on the seams.

He accidentally tore a piece of the splendiferous coat on a nail. The rips and tears on the coat grew larger with time. There were holes and breaks at the shoulder from when he struggled with thieves on the road as they tried to steal his coat.

Still, all these battles, all these escapes, all these rescues had taught the man much. He would never have become the man he was—strong and kind and steadfast—had it not been for the splendiferous coat in which he walked.

Finally, from sitting, standing, bending, and laying, the bottom of the coat wore so thin, you could hold it up and tell where the sun hung in the sky.

With his knife, the man cut away at the bottom of the coat, and he made a handsome jacket from it that ran from his shoulders to his waist. Still, it was a bit ragged. Yet, it stayed that way for a long, long time. The man wore it on all his adventures. He sailed the seas in it. He flew the skies in it. The splendiferous coat had become his splendiferous jacket. In his jacket, he felt loved. He felt secure. When he reached into the pockets of the jacket, the pockets still fed him.

Through his many adventures, the jacket

began to wear again. As he himself grew older, his jacket grew more threadbare. Soon, the sleeves were in ribbons. So it was that the man met an able seamstress at the crossroads. She wore a hat woven with emeralds, rubies, and diamonds.

"My good man, " said the seamstress, "your jacket is in tatters. Here, purchase one of mine." The seamstress showed the man her wagon, full of fine garments, woven in gold and silver and bronze.

187

"Oh how much I should desire to purchase this one," the man said as he touched a sparkling golden coat with his hands. It was dazzling. But, alas, the adventuresome man had no ability to pay. But, more importantly, the man loved his tattered jacket for it had walked and sailed and flown the many miles with him. It was part of him.

At the crossroads, the seamstress with the sparkling goods and the man parted ways. The man journeyed onward by himself.

In the morning when he awakened, the ribbony sleeves of the jacket fell away as leaves from the autumn tree. The man was left with a splendiferous vest that ran over his shoulders, down his chest, and to his hips. He remained of good humor and good will for the vest served his purposes but not as well as before.

When he slept, the vest covered him, almost. When he was lonely, he pulled it tighter and it comforted him, more or less. In the pockets, there was still the food he needed to continue his quests.

As he adventured on the roads, the vest became more worn, still. Soon, it was hanging from his shoulders in rags. He said to himself, "I will use it still, and I will fashion this part of the vest as a sash that runs over my shoulders and runs to the waist." That is what he did. There was still one pocket over to the side. When he searched into it, there was still a little food. When he slept, he was comforted in the middle by the sash. In truth, he did not always sleep well for he was not as warm as he used to be. When he felt lonely, there was not much he could pull toward himself. But, there was enough.

One night, as he was sleeping in his raggedy sash, the sash seemed to take on a life of its own. It began to unravel. First, one thread broke and curled upward. Then, another. The threads made no sound but to open and break like the curling petals to a blooming spring flower. Suddenly, out of the break in the sash, out leapt the old man's luminous soul, which raced up and out into the evening air in boundless joy.

189

The soul looked back at the world, without regret. The joyous soul looked back at the splendiferous coat, now but a splendiferous sash, that had been its home for so many years. There had been so many marvelous adventures. There had been so many lessons. The soul had learned so much from walking in the splendiferous coat.

Then the soul lifted higher until it joined the sparkling stars that, along with the moon, made the night bright.